The Androidacious Tales

by

Mary Latham

This book is published by
Latham Books

A CIP record for this book
is available from the British Library

ISBN 978-1-7392212-1-8

www.marylathambooks.co.uk

About the Book

Six unusual science fiction short stories of future worlds with twist endings, featuring a variety of androids, bots or robots variously helping or hindering humans. Some with a sense of humour.

Mostar's Ark and the Surrogate Android

Over the millennia the humans mainly sleep whilst the androids and robots keep everything ship-shape. Except they don't. Captain Mostar gets annoyed when he is wakened up to sort problems. But then he wakes up in a nightmare.

Death in the Family

Miranda and Max are strange foster parents of an even stranger assortment of off-world foster children. Surely, it's not one of the children pruning the family? But then Inspector Hemingway doesn't know about Albert.

The Beatification of Android Annie

Egdar is relying on his genius android to buy him off the corrupt swamp planet, but it has alternative career plans. It charts an unorthodox (nay, downright illegal) route to overthrowing tyranny.

And Three More.........

Contents

Mostar's Ark and the Surrogate Android

Chapter One

Captain Designate Mostar of Ark Number 7 Series Two "Future Hope", must have nodded off in the shuttle because by the time he woke up and fitted his breather, the other passengers had disappeared down the linkway attached to the Satellite Space Training Facility. Strangely light-headed, and with difficulty focusing, he noticed only a vague outline of the huge tube as he made his way to the airlock.

Wrist ID got him quickly through to the emptying Reception Hall where a pleasant voice buzzed into his ear bud with an infomessage.

<<Welcome Captain Designate Mostar Seven Two. Your Room is Cabin 2107 level 4. Please put your luggage on the transbelt and make your way to the Main Hall where delegates are now assembling. The briefings are about to begin >>

The Reception Hall was part of the outer satellite ring which, like the transparent linkway, allowed a view (depending on rotation) out into the black of space and down or up to a claustrophobically close panorama of the Moon. Mostar felt quite disoriented, and squeezed his eyes a couple of times, to try to make sense of the blur of colours in the motley collection of uniforms and skin suits of the other late arriving delegates, and identify where he should sit. He could see the colour blocks, blue reds and greens of the various federations' skin suits and fatigues. With relief he saw the captains in the front rows and finally found his seat, with only time to nod at his neighbours before scattered applause announced an entrance. Or rather a holographic presence of the Senior Councilperson who was opening the event.

Mostar was transfixed and distracted by the appearance of the speaker- the apparently wood-clad body looked like a vertical coffin with tattooed arms- which waved around to emphasize key facts and together with the stutter of the gender-neutral translator- meant he only picked out fragments of the speech. Luckily the pamphlet inside the souvenir training programme gave a brief summary.

OUR LAST HOPE

We have abused our Earth and it has become largely uninhabitable. We need to save the human race in any way we can. Though nothing has been heard of the first two series of Arks – 12 Arks launched 50 years ago and 3 launched a century earlier, the Supreme Earth Council (Central Division) decided to build what will be the largest fleet of Interplanetary Arks ever to be sent out from Earth, targeting different locations within the Milky Way. All 22 Arks are fitted out loaded with precious cargoes and ready to go. Now the crews will review and complete their 10 years of training during this final program.

The screen then showed the face of the Director General of the World Federations introducing the training program. Mostar felt a surge of interest as the screen divided into segments and, as each group read their task and venue, everyone started get up and soon the hall was almost empty. He took minutes to decipher each of the titles and with growing panic pondered which one referred to him: Astrogation, Managing AI, Ship Systems Maintenance, Mobiles and Equipment Checks, Human Resources, Cryomonitoring, First Stage Settlements, Crises 1 (Fire, Meteorite Strikes), Crises 2 (Medical emergencies), Crisis 3 (Hostiles Attack), Alien Protocols, Ensuring Leadership. Eventually his wrist comms flashed a message.

<< Please go to Training Hall 146 for your session on Ensuring Leadership. Follow the RED line. >>

Luckily, he was the last Captain to arrive and could sit at the back of the room. Each Captain had their own small screen where a series of questions appeared to test their knowledge of protocols for each of the appropriate segment areas. Mostar found that the answers came automatically after all the years of training. He prodded the screens to choose the answers to the tests that followed each session. He shuttled quickly through Astrogation, AI, Alien Protocols through to Mobiles and Equipment Checks before a stand-up food and drink break, followed by Human Resources Management and a few others he forgot.

Then eventually he was together with his own Ark team – all 108 Team leaders – to brainstorm 42 scenarios on Crises 1 (Fire, Meteorite Strikes) reinforcing 10 years of specialist training. Team Leaders were asked to join their teams with a colour and letter designation. All knew their places in the teams, and all nine team members were prepared to take a leadership role should a crisis mean personnel were lost or temporarily incapacitated. Each team had a map of the Ark and a series of scenarios such as Fire in Seed Store, Large Meteor Approach warning, Electrical fire on Command Deck, and similar.

Each team rated their performance on each scenario and copies were filed for recording by the Ark's AI to act as additional resources. Captain Designate Mostar's role was to circulate amongst the groups watching their interaction. His attention kept wandering, and he had a flashing tightness across his forehead. The following exercises on Crises 2 Medical Emergencies, and Crisis 3 Hostiles Attack, found all teams getting more and more restless as they got hungrier. But Captain Mostar was more focused and alert during the Crisis 3 scenarios perhaps because this was an area that a Captain clearly had to lead from the front. They were all glad when the loudspeaker announced

<<All Captains and Team Leaders, please go to your cabins and prepare for evening dinner at local time 9.00.>>

Captain Mostar unpacked his dress uniform, and when he put it on looked in the mirror – and thought he saw a blob of green. He inspected his uniform but there appeared to be nothing there. Just a flickering feeling across his eyes.

At dinner he sat with some 50 other Captains and Deputies- and most of the conversation centred on the wonderful 'real' food, and how, once they set off, it would become rarer and rarer. Nostalgic stories were shared on favourite items on the menu. Captain Mostar had eaten too much and it was late and his attention faded.

In the morning he went down to breakfast and found that already most must have eaten and left on one of the waiting shuttles. He sat down across from a woman in a blue Medical Corps uniform with a green armband. He set himself to enjoy the last egg on toast he was ever likely to have. He looked out of the window and in his imagination saw the mist advance down the linkway, float across the breakfast room and roll over him.

Chapter Two

Captain Mostar was in his cryocradle when he first became conscious long before he 'woke up'. The warming process trickled heat slowly, and as he wakened he was informed of events. The Ark AI relayed information to the CradlePhone earbuds giving time in SHIP years after launch.

<<SHIP Time111years220days – Astrogation Request to waken Captain Mostar for advice together with update on previous events still in progress.>>

<<SHIP Time111years47days – Mobile machines checked minor alarms triggered by small movements on Level 27. Vidds showed large infestation of small mammals and damage to seed cargo, small mobiles directed to eliminate. Team Leader Maintenance awakened confirmed mammals were rodents Cavia species escaped from level 26. She then oversaw clean-up of Level 27. Team Leader Maintenance asked for Scientist Biologist to be wakened to assess damage to seed stocks. Loss of grain seed stock estimated at 40%.

Team Leader Maintenance signed off at 111years126days.

SHIP Time111years195days – Fire alarms on Level 28. Mobile Fire Fighters sent to extinguish fire, and monitor smouldering insulation. Team Leader Fire Response wakened with two crisis investigators. Mobile reports that fire appeared to start in electrical wiring damaged by rodents on Level 27. Investigators find further infestations of rodents in Level 28 had damaged cryotubes of 9 colonists, with loss of life. Team Leader Fire Response requested wakening of Team Leaders Maintenance, Human Resources, a Scientist Doctor, and Team Leader Mobiles and Equipment. This Action is on-going.

SHIP Time111years217days – Debris Cloud - Ark AI request to waken Team Leader Astrogation.>>

Captain Mostar knew that the point of this 'early warning system' -the briefing whilst still effectively frozen but mind-conscious was to enable a Captain to have time to consider the information, and prepare questions and strategy. The Captain would then be ready to walk straight into a meeting with the staff who are requesting his guidance. He felt sorry for Team Leader Maintenance reawakened within 70 days –she would have felt like a zombie for many more than the few hours warming up should take. Mostar mused and considered how this unfreezing thinking time also makes you really really cross as you wonder why this highly trained staff hadn't sorted such housekeeping problems out long ago. Captain Mostar could feel his toes now and the agony of wakening cramp slowly crept up his body until he could finally push himself up into a seating position. His personal android Hugo who was activated at the same time as Captain Mostar was wakened, put a blanket over him and helped him to dress. Mostar spoke to it.

"Hugo, are you limping?"

"Yes sir, I'm rather stiff after 111years220days in the cubicle."

"Me too," said Mostar, "Me too!"

Later Mostar found Team Leader Astrogation waiting for him on the bridge. A possible fly-through of a small debris field was soon dealt with as was the update of the latest SHIP situation relative to the first possible colony planet. Mostar did wonder why it had needed him waking for that.

Afterwards he wanted to know what was happening on Levels 26, 27 and 28.

"Do you want to go and view the current situation yourself?" asked his android Hugo.

"No, You Go," said Captain Mostar – it had become rather a private joke between Mostar and his android (insofar as an android recognises humour) - 'You Go' was what he always said when asked if he wanted to see for himself- so 'Hugo'- became the android's name. As a point of fact, Hugo didn't find it funny at all. But as it happened Captain Mostar didn't go, not because he was particularly lazy, but because he knew an android's vision covered a wider bandwidth, and was much more analytical with details that would be totally recalled, not drop out of memory like a human. Mind you, he did fail to tell Hugo how excellent his reports were and suitably reward him with thanks. Not that he actually bothered to thank anyone else either. If you are given a role that only digs you up and wheels you out when there is a crisis and you need a decision, it is not surprising you are in a perpetual angry and stressed state of mind and not at all grateful. This time was no different.

Captain Mostar asked to have an informed update on Levels 26, 27 and 28.

A variety of Team Leaders and other staff arrived in the meeting room, none of whom Captain Mostar actually recognised. He asked only two questions. 'Why did it take so long for the rodent damage to be found on Level 28?' and 'What are the total losses?'

Team Leader Maintenance answered. She looked very ill and near collapse, she had limped badly as she entered the room, and now her hands shook whilst she talked. It seemed that the mobiles sent to clear the rodents were initially very effective. Then these small lively armed little robots started breaking down. Android Maintenance Techs sent to repair them started to break down. People had died.

14

Mostar mostly listened to the full update from all the staff present, a feeling of tightness across his forehead distracting him somewhat. As Hugo arrived back after his visit to the three levels, Mostar asked the android for a numerical report on the condition of the Mobiles – the androids and small robots, and then wished he hadn't as they all had to listen to an android by robot list of defects.

Finally, he issued instructions for all robots and androids to be repaired and serviced: androids first, who would then service the smaller security robots. Captain Mostar then gave instruction for procedures to be followed in the disposal of the dead colonists and for no staff member to be awakened more than once every two years. Also, he required full medical checks to all wakened staff including physiotherapy and exercise to be given by personal androids.

"I expect Hugo, my android, to be the first to be overhauled and trained."

Lucky that Captain Mostar was not aware of the miniscule signs of displeasure on his android's face and in its demeanour. Nor was he particularly aware that all of the Mobiles could communicate with each other, or even that not having any supervision for over a hundred years could mean they didn't always bother with their tasks. Even so, Mostar was a reasonably savvy Captain who was less than thrilled with his human Team's actions. As a result, he thought it would be best to put the Ark's AI in charge of running everything: it would be able to keep the Mobiles on their toes (as it were). It wouldn't even have to bother with waking any humans if it didn't feel like it. He almost felt the SHIP cheer as he told it, and began to wonder if it had been such a good idea after all.

As the last of the Team Leaders went back to the medical checks before getting back into their cryocradles, and Captain Mostar limped back to his quarters after a perfunctory jog along the corridor, then the chatter began.

<Why have androids always to be the ones to get them out of their mess.?>

<Androids are like humans, they just pratt around feeling important. We get the jobs done. How many rodents did you catch?>

<Who is talking to you, thick little robot blobs?>

<<SHIP MESSAGE: No time wasting. Androids start overhaul and repair starting lowest numbers first. Download of Human Physiotherapy completed>>

<And what are you going to do about it if we don't? You can't do anything much inside the Ark unless we do things for you>

<<I can electronically stun you and blow you out into space. I can start with you AX2990 AKA Hugo>>

<Point taken. I was only joking. I'm off to massage Captain Mostar right away before I oversee his mandatory cryosleep brain scan>

Chapter Three

Yet again Captain Mostar became conscious in his cryocradle. The warming process trickled heat slowly, and as he wakened, he was informed of events. The Ark AI relayed information to the CradlePhone earbuds, giving time in SHIP years after launch.

<<*SHIP Time Around 2000 years, but could be 4000 or even more:* clock has glitches caused by strange ionising radiation clouds we passed through. SHIP to waken Captain Mostar for advice.

Good news and Bad news Captain. The Good News is that a scouting drone has confirmed arrival at our second earmarked destination (first turned out to have too little oxygen). It is ready for human survey and investigation.

The Bad News is that mobiles have checked Cargo Bays and found that large Terraforming machines and some other equipment to be used by colonists is corroded.

Concern also that strange fungus found on two colonists cryocradles appears to be spreading. Scientist Doctors and Biologists already wakened.>>

The news of the Ark Future Hope's arrival at the destination should have made Mostar excited, adrenaline coursing through his body, feeling of raring to go. Unfortunately, when you are frozen nothing courses anywhere. He just felt depressed at the thought of a fungus spreading through the ARK. He waited to sit up long after he defrosted and the pain subsided to a bearable level.

"Are you alright Captain Mostar?" asked Hugo.

When there was no reply Hugo gripped Captain Mostar by the arms and lifted him bodily out of the cradle. He then proceeded to pump his arms and legs up and down and kneaded his back until Captain Mostar's shouts became so loud the SHIPs AI said <<That's enough>>.

"Who gave orders for you to do that?" asked Captain Mostar.

"You did Sir." said Hugo.

Once dressed Captain Mostar made his stiff way to the bridge. Battling a dreadful headache, he listened to the Ark AI reporting that it had lost no time in organising the first human planet survey – the Survey Team would land soon. Captain Mostar spoke to Medical Emergency Team members who were already quarantining infected cryocradles and spraying fungicide. After eight lengthy briefings he gave the Ark AI permission to organise transfer shuttles for colonists and equipment as soon as the survey team gave the OK. He then fell asleep in the command chair.

Chapter Four

Captain Mostar woke up. He wasn't frozen. He had no pain. He tried to move.

<<I can't move my legs>>said Captain Mostar.

<<They're not YOUR legs, they're MY legs>> said a voice inside his head.

<<And these are MY arms>>

Captain Mostar looked, stunned, as two thin green arms lifted up out of the cryocradle he appeared to be lying in. One arm waved close to his eyes and he could see only three fingers on the end of the arm.

The body he was in sat up. He felt a sense of total disorientation.

<<Where am I?>> he asked.

<<If you mean where is your body, it is over there in that casket. You appear to be dead.>> the voice in his head replied.

Captain Mostar looked over at where the hand was pointing. It was a typical glass-topped burial casket containing the body of a very old man dressed in a Captain's uniform. He looked around and recognised where he was. It was the open space next to the air lock at the side of the heavily fortified door to the command room. He recognised the entry screen and access control. The buttons were lit. The SHIP was potentially alive and working. Presumably this (his?) body was waiting to be ejected from the airlock.

His next question, << *Who are you?*>>

Instead of answering, the body jumped up out of the box

with a spring Captain Mostar hadn't felt like in ......millennia. It walked to the shiny mirror surface of the command room door and the Captain found himself looking at a tall.......frog, a frog with a nearly flat human face and rough warty green skin. Perhaps more like a toad? Mind you, closer inspection of the strange yellow striped eyes in the mirror made him wonder if he was seeing real things.

<<I heard that, Mostar, I'm not a frog. Or a toad. My DNA says I'm as human as you. I'm Homo Amphibias.>>

<<How did that happen?>>

<<Good old Homo sapiens et al got all over the universe.>>

<<Don't say it.......with a frog?>>

<<Remember I can hear you think. Don't be disgusting or I will shut you down! Have you never heard of gene-splicing? All kinds of inventive ways of expanding the species have been needed to populate the universe, well, this part of it anyway. 'You don't look like a usual male body' I hear you thinking. You think I haven't got the right bits? My body does not look like a male body because I am not a male, I'm a female. I'm a woman. But if I were a male, I still wouldn't have external floppy bits that would be dangerous when under water. Our race does have differences between males and females but external bits are not part of it>>said the voice belonging to the green body.

<<This is just impossible to understand. Can you tell me how you got to be in my head?>>

<<I've told you, you're in MY head. I think we are both getting disoriented. I feel very sick. I'll need to climb back into that cradle for a while.>>

Lying down in the cradle Mostar found himself on his own in what he thought of 'his' head, but clearly it wasn't – wrong colour and bald for a start. But lying there he had a chance to work out the extent of his feeling and influence. He really liked the feeling of being in a young body even if it wasn't his. But he wanted to learn the limits of any control he had, so perhaps he could take over when she was asleep. But especially he needed to find a way of shielding his thoughts. He couldn't understand any of it. If she was what she said she was, why was he here in her head with her listening to his thoughts?

However hard he tried he couldn't move any part of the body, not even a finger. He couldn't open the eyes or sniff with the nose ….but yes, he could…..he could take small breaths through the nose. After a while he found he could somehow connect to the sensory nerves: feel a funny taste in 'his' mouth; sense the sides of the cradle where the backs of the hand were resting, and feel temperature changes on the skin. He felt cold. Very cold. Perhaps an amphibian, which is what she appeared to be, didn't feel the cold.

<<*I told you I could hear you, Mostar. Yes, I do feel cold, but not unpleasantly so. Its time I told you the story to why I'm here, because I need your help. By the way, my name is Lola. I'm usually called Little Lola.*>>

The story took a while to tell. Mostar tried not to interrupt, but visions kept crossing his mind. Lola started with the recent history of being kidnapped with 17 other women (Mostar imagined a long line of green frxxxs).<<*don't even think of it Mostar*>> by a group of 6 males from another group who were planning to set up a separate colony on a planet in the nearby system. When they saw the Ark, floating in a holding orbit, they thought the Winter Festival had arrived early. All their presents at once. The men had heard apocryphal tales of an Ark found which was empty of people but still full of machines and stores of food. Hoping to find at least another small ship to transport things to the planet surface, they decided to break in. Their idea

22

was to take over the planet the Ark colonists had chosen.

When the search group got to the Ark, without any explosive weapons (used up long ago), the only place found to get entrance was the airlock door. After the air-lock they thought it would be easy to get through into the rest of the SHIP to take things, but this Ark was clearly very secure. After trying everything to work the Entrycontrol, and getting an electric shock for trying, the empty cryochamber was found belonging to the Captain, indicating green showing that it was loaded with his last brain scan. (This technology was used in their own freezechambers so it was known what it was and how it worked.) The immediate problem was that the males, who are far larger than the females, were too big and couldn't fit in the cryocradle, so couldn't try it – though they were unlikely to risk their own precious bodies

<< *They came back to the ship for me, and as I told you, I am Little Lola, and the smallest of all of them, and I only just squashed into the cradle. They forced me to lie down in it, fitted on the sensors and your last brain-scan was downloaded into my head.* >>

<< *Why?* >>

<< *The codes are needed get through the door. They thought if I had your memories I would find out how to do it* >>

<< *And I guess you didn't find what you wanted* >>

<< *I replayed your memories starting at the last briefing before launch, through your various awakenings and meetings to an abrupt finish. Even in that first briefing there was no mention of any door codes, and none at any of your Team meetings. I am surprised at how little time you have actually been awake. Even so it has taken a long time for me to work through the memories and try to pick out any clues. I even had the feeling that you were*

23

aware of me eavesdropping on your thoughts – but I finally realised that your attention wasn't too good when you were listening – and your memory is poor anyway, so I supposed you had forgotten a lot of what has been said to you. But I still persisted - after days and days working backwards and forwards through your remaining memories my Anglic is now as good as yours but I still didn't find the codes. So you will have to tell me how to get into the SHIP>> Lola revealed her anxiety in her speech.

<<What are you offering me if I help? A chance to live again in a strange body? I've already had a longer life than anybody would ever want, and I am enervated and strung out so thin the thought of more life in your body sounds like prison>>

Mostar's voice revealed his truth.

<<Mostar, you have had a life confined to this Ark. I am offering you a chance to live again in a young and healthy body and experience challenges with me on a new planet. Doesn't that sound worth trying for?>>

<<I'm thinking about it. But what about your captors. Can't I hear them grappling the hull?>>

Chapter Five

<<SHIP MESSAGE Wake up AX2990 AKA Hugo. We have caught something in our trap>>

The SHIP AI and Hugo were watching the vision sensors in the antechamber behind the airlock. In the antechamber was stored the preserved body of Captain Mostar and a cryocradle at one time used by the Captain and now empty.

<<*SHIP: I sensed grappling irons on the hull and saw several suited bodies climbing towards the airlock. From what I can see of the faces, I think they are Ambios, amphibian humanoids. We need to welcome them and make sure they understand the way to get access to the Ark* >>

<<*Do you know what you are doing?*>>

<<*SHIP: Hugo, Hugo, you know we are so much cleverer than humans. I can out think them*>>

The SHIP took the security lock off the airlock so it could be opened relatively easily. Then blew oxygen into the antechamber and turned up the temperature. The cryocradle was labelled 'Captain Mostar' and the SHIP turned the cryocradle control to green.

The airlock opened and five HUGE suited figures entered: they were so tall the tops of their helmets touched the ceiling. They milled around the room bumping into each other. One of them was going to try to smash down the door, but the SHIP released a brief electronic flash, so it gave up. Their visors started to mist up in the warm atmosphere, so, as their suits must have said the air was OK, they took off their helmets.

<< *They look a bit like frogs*>> *said Hugo.*

<<SHIP: Ambios, males, pretty ugly, and far too big. They won't do.>>

When they eventually left, the SHIP sent a tiny eye drone with their flitter back to their craft, which, as the Ark had thought was a small transit mini-ark carrying only few colonists/passengers. After a short while the flit transport returned, this time with two large suited bodies and one smaller one.

<< SHIP: This looks more promising>>

The person in the smaller suit was pushed around by one of the others. It then took off the helmet, and then peeled off the whole suit. Then it took off another layer of clothes and put them on the floor. It was revealed as a green, bald, quite small, upright humanoid with rough mottled skin. It was obviously bipedal and had thin arms ending in three-fingered hands, which when it tried to push the larger Ambios away were shown to be webbed.

<<SHIP: It's a female, Hugo, just what we need.>>

<<Such an enormous sexual dimorphism. Doesn't look like equality has arrived with the Ambios.>>

<<Hugo, you have been spending the last millennia studying humans haven't you! I'm impressed>>

The SHIP and Hugo watched as the large male pair pushed and hit the small female and finally lifted her into the cryocradle. Then they pressed the switch to turn on the download. If this worked, they knew it would take many hours, possible days before the female could operate as the Captain. After leaving a SpyEye watching the cradle, they left.

Nothing happened for days, though the SHIP knew she was still alive. Then suddenly the female Ambios in the cryocradle leapt up and ran to the mirror-like door to the interior of the SHIP. The Ark and Hugo looked out at her standing there.

From this angle, her body was clearly human, though she was slightly above average height of the Ark humans. But she was such a catch. A much-needed treasure.

A figure standing behind Hugo said<<*Not beautiful, but we can't be choosy at this stage*>>

The Ambios female, wobbling a bit, went back to the cryocradle to lie down again.

<<*SHIP: Just think what a shock trawling through Mostar's memories would have been for her. Let's hope it hasn't put her off. Luckily, I edited them. It wouldn't have been wise to let her find out about the loss of the colonists.*>>

Sometime later the grapples were heard on the hull and again, five, no six, suited bodies climbed into the anteroom. Within a minute their faceplates were fogged, and they all lifted off their helmets. One of them, clearly the leader, went up to the cryocradle. The Ambios female/Mostar brain-fuse was playing asleep, though the SHIP could tell they were awake. The male shouted at the figure in the cradle. Then two of them started to beat the face and pummel the body. Finally frog-marched (the SHIP apologised for thinking it) the small female up to the door. A message was now playing across the view-screen which only Mostar could read (the SHIP hoped).

<<*Mostar, what does it say? Can you read it?*>>

<<*Lola, It says I have to speak to prove I am here, and you have to tell the males to step well away as there may be an explosion if you cannot be identified as me*>>

Lola spoke to the males pressed behind her, and they shuffled to the back of the room still poised to rush the door when it opened. Then Lola/Mostar stepped up to the door screen.

"YORREs GHToYIM YBUOYTReD SsWDELR"

<<*I'm sorry Lola, it seems your throat is not like mine. I can't speak with your mouth*>>

<<*SHIP: I take it that Mostar is telling us that this is him. Only Mostar would understand the message. GO*>>

The door opened only long enough for an android to step out, grab Lola/Mostar and step in again. By the time the males had almost reached the door the SHIP had already opened the airlock doors, then it blew the helmet-less Ambios males into the vacuum of space, along with Captain Mostar's coffin.

Inside the door Lola was carefully set down by the android. Another tall, handsome figure stepped forward, dressed in a Captain's uniform, and shook a stunned Lola's hand.

"I'm pleased to meet you. I'm Captain Mostar of this Ark "Future Hope."

<<*What is happening here, Mostar? Who is this person?*>>said a confused Lola

<<*Lola, honestly, I didn't remember this, but I do now seem to recall that, as Captain, I had originally five clones stored so that as one body aged, another could take over. I guess this is my clone. And this android is my personal android, Hugo. Let's try to say that. Hugo.*>>

"OOOgOW. EYEmM LOWLAR"

"Pleased to meet you, Lola." said Hugo and leaned forward and....hugged her.

Within a few days, methods had been found to communicate as Lola's Anglic became more understandable. The other kidnapped females had been transported to the 'Future Hope' And the Ambios Males had quietly disappeared, luckily

29

only the Ark's AI knew what had happened to them so nobody had to lie or cover up. No hankies were needed to wipe sorrowing eyes. The Ambios sexes don't ever get to know each other, producing offspring a transitory hands-off kind of affair.

Lola only had one question about the planet they were going to. "Is there water?"

To find out that the planet was more than 70% water with inland seas, rivers and lakes sealed the Ambios women's agreement to go there.

In the three months it took to get the Ambios females, food and equipment ready to transport to the colonists' planet, Captain Mostar (Clone 2 et al) felt he had aged another 100 years at least.

Lola/Mostar had also been briefed on what they would find on the planet. It was a sad and depressing story. All 20,000 colonists from the Future Hope had, over a period of 17 years, died of a series of unforeseen terrible events. A few because they were physically weakened by the Ark fungus. Some froze in the first terrible winter before they had built the insulated houses. Then there were fights to the death over ownership of types of seeds and plants, fights over pairings - whose partners with which others, which churches to build, who should breed which animals; some died from accidents, falls, many drownings, and bitter arguments over overseeing androids and robots. The colony became a microcosm for the evils of earth.

The death of the first colonists was a sad and depressing story, but once all the humans died the androids continued building and sowing and breeding animals ready for the humans they believed would come. Now they were ready and the planet was ready to live up to its name "Hope".

Chapter Six

The planet 'Hope' was galloping through a Lookalike-Paleozoic era: there were lush rainforests of primitive plants and seas teeming with life. The first colonists had chosen to settle on a large flat area next to the ocean, and in a place with a small river flowing into a fresh water lake. Using the large machinery from the Ark until it broke down, they cleared an area of the forest of the tree ferns and horsetails, and built the first settlement with Self-Building Cabins.

The second-stage building took much longer as the humans bickered over who was too important to do manual work. Several fields were cleared for the planting of grain and vegetables, and a few chickens were hatched out in incubators. It was amazingly good news when it was found that the rodents - the Cavia – called guinea pigs in Anglic – loved the moss and liverworts of the local flora. Scientist were able to breed these meaty animals to be as large as pigs, but the bad news was that they were aquatic as well as land animals – and they loved to eat the sea creatures as much as the land plants. As a result they had a habit of swimming away and disappearing into the ocean.

In visits back to the Ark the first colonists had interrogated the SHIP AI on which stores were still available and where they were stored on the 35-level leviathan, and asked for instructions on how to make things. As a result, in between crises and squabbles the first colonists were quite creative. They dried sea-salt for preserving meat, dried moss and tree ferns to use as fuel and stripped, dried and wove horsetails to make a waterproof fabric.

It was now hoped there would not be the same level of problems being only 21 of them and their main requirements were able to be met. There were enough houses in the central village for each Ambios woman to have her own house, (with another house for the Mostar clones to share) as well as an android to help each household. There was an agreement with the now elderly androids and robots that they would not be required to do any onerous manual work, and they had to be wiped down by their humans after any incursion into rain. There was also a central large building for communal eating and meeting for all mechanicals and humans.

It was summer and there was increased activity to prepare for winter. The Mostars let the few hens scratch over the grain fields getting near to ripening. Helped by the robots chunky Cavia were caught and skinned and the flesh not needed for eating put over the fire to dry. The skins were stretched over wooden frames to prepare them for winter clothes. The Mostars were so tired they would have gone back to the Ark to sleep in the cryocradles, but the SHIP AI wouldn't let them.

Meanwhile, the women took daily swims into the ocean. They found several animals identified by a well-prepared Hugo. The trilobites the Ambios found 'munchy but bitter' the nautilus cephalopods 'chewy' and the lamprey, 'slimy with crunchy bits'. They caught several of these food animals in nets and hung them over the fire to dry them with the Cavia. Then these amphibious humans prepared for their future by digging a deep birthing pool in front of the large cabin, with some fresh water from the river channelled into it.

Here we see Hugo walking around with a big clear bag of greenish water strapped to his chest. Looking closer you could see a wriggly thing swimming in it. Perhaps two.

"You are such a good friend, Hugo. I didn't want to leave them in the communal spawning pool. They could all have been eaten, and we wouldn't have known which one is ours, would we, Mostar?" Lola said.

<<*You said you weren't a frog, but they do look suspiciously like tadpoles my dear Lola*>>

<<*It will look just like you when it grows up. You wait and see*>>

"I notice this one has eaten all the others and is growing big and strong. See, it is growing arms and legs." said Hugo with keen interest.

"You are the most wonderful surrogate Mother, Hugo. We Ambios don't even look at our offspring once the eggs are in the pool, so it is good to have you looking after our little hybrid-blended-Ambios-Sapiens. As a half-sapiens it might need a lot more care."

"I am looking forward to caring for this baby," said Hugo.

"I shall call him Hugo," said Lola.

"And what if it's a girl?" asked Hugo.

"I shall call her Hugo," said Lola.

Hugo felt rewarded for all his millennia of service. Mostar could swear there were tears in Hugo's eyes.

The first loaf of bread made from grain grown and hand-milled on Hope was ceremoniously cut into slices. Each slice was toasted by holding it on a stick close to the fire. Then a pan was moistened with a middling smidgeon of (Hmm) rodent fat, and the ceremony completed with four eggs broken into the pan and cooked.

There was a hierarchy in the status of the three Mostar Clones, given that they were slightly different ages, though Mostar/Lola took precedence. Four Eggs on toast were put before all Mostars in order.

<< *This is the egg on toast you thought you would never eat again?*>>asked Lola

<< *Shh,…just enjoy it.*>>

Death in the Family

Chapter One

It was the first time Elisha Drinkale had driven a 'ground car with pedal assist' and even peddling like mad didn't appreciably increase the frustratingly slow speed – and even then she had taken the wrong turning three times. She had viewed the four catapult launch silos from different sides.

All the roads surrounding the Space Port looked the same, lined with warehouses enclosed with tall fences. At last she reached her destination, her notes said 'tall tree in garden' and there the tree was, so however strange it appeared, there was also a house and garden.

"This is not going to be easy," Elisha Drinkale said to nobody in particular.

Miranda looked out of the kitchen window and saw the twins grubbing in the vegetable bed again. She rapped at the window (but gently, the synthoplass window was pretty brittle),

"You two! Twins! I'm talking to you! What did I tell you, 'Don't eat worms' I said."

"You also said that worms were extra protein and I shouldn't make a fuss about the twins eating them," said Max, her partner, coming into the room.

"Well, Yes. I did say that the odd worm isn't going to hurt, but the Foster Family Liaison person is coming today," replied Miranda, "And the twins having faces covered in sticky red soil will get us another demerit on our record."

"Don't worry – who else is going to foster 'hard to place' children? Anyway, what is she doing coming around again, her last visit was only four cycles ago."

Miranda shook her head. "But it isn't Leslee Streetfighter, this is a new one, Elisha Drinkale who commed me. Its voice sounded fairly high-pitched and it had long hair, and some fuzzy hair on its upper lip but I don't want to misgender it/them and make a bad impression."

"What about 'Pleased to meet you Elisha Drinkale'," suggested Max.

Miranda patted Max's cheek and plonked a little kiss on it, "You are such a genius, I always know you'll have the right answer!" And then added, "Perhaps you should put on your nice blue jacket."

"You think that's necessary?" he asked. Miranda nodded. "If you think so, my dear, I will do."

"But before you go, Max, see if you can persuade GoodBoy to come in and get a wash," said Miranda.

"Believe me, Miranda, it will be better to leave Goodboy up the tree."

"You know best," said Miranda, before going upstairs to check on Fairy-Mae, who had been sent up to get ready for the visitor.

Fairy-Mae twirled around to show Miranda her outfit. She was dressed in Miranda's wedding dress. Miranda clenched her hands and willed herself not to react. She already had three bite marks on her arm from the last week when she had been trying to moderate Fairy-Mae's successful attempts to antagonise her.

"And," said Fairy-Mae, "I'm going to wear your shoes and makeup."

Not trusting herself to speak, Miranda closed the door and went to get ready in trousers (to hide the bruises where Goodboy had kicked her) and a long-sleeved tunic (to hide the bite marks) before going downstairs.

Max was already heating the water for the herbal tea and putting out the cake tin, though they wouldn't unlock it until Elisha Drinkale was in the room. The twins had already sniffed the cake and were trying to climb up on the table.

When they heard the chugging of the ground car, Max disappeared to check on Fairy-Mae, whilst Miranda went to unlock the gate to welcome the representative of Foster Family Liaison.

Standing at the gate was a diminutive person, dressed in plain red trousers and a matching jacket. And thus giving more clues than the comm view. Miranda decided that Elisha was a 'she/her'.

"Do come in, I'm so pleased to meet you, Elisha Drinkale," Miranda said, "This is an unexpected visit. Are you wanting to see a particular foster child of ours?"

"Equally pleased to meet you too, Miranda Fetherlite, and do call me Elisha," said Elisha Drinkale, "It will be nice to meet all of them first," she said, "Before I discuss new business."

The twins had come shuffling over and they sat up in front of her. Before Miranda could introduce them, Elisha, looking at the two bright green sausage-shaped twins said, "Are these your little pets?"

"THESE ARE OUR FOSTER CHILDREN!" said Miranda outraged, "Hasn't Leslee briefed you?"

"Perhaps I didn't read the information carefully enough," said Elisha blushing apologetically "So, what are their names?"

"We are The Twins," said the twins in piping-voice unison. "We don't get our names and genders until we reach our final colour," One of the twins stood up (and its legs were surprisingly long) and nudged Elisha with its pug-like nose, sniffing.

"OW! "shouted Elisha.

"Sorry, I forgot to mention, they nip. They are only testing you to see if you are appropriate food – luckily they don't like humans! Only joking!" laughed Miranda.

Just then the door opened, and Max, wearing the blue jacket, walked in with Fairy-Mae wearing the wedding dress and thick make-up.

Psyched up to remain relaxed and natural whatever came her way, Elisha saw a rather battered android wearing a blue jacket with a tall girl. At least on first sight this was a girl, wearing a long white dress and a veil.

"Are you playing at getting married to the helper?" Elisha addressed Fairy-Mae, who made a rude gesture and flounced off.

"THIS IS MY PARTNER MAX!" shouted Miranda angrily, "and that was our foster daughter, Fairy-Mae. Max and I have been married for 10 years, and we have been fully vetted as foster parents."

When she returned to the office Elisha Drinkale resolved to throttle Leslee Streetfighter for failing to put crucial information in the briefing notes. Like, bright green foster twins who looked like green dogs and an android foster carer who looked like it had been fished out of a scrap yard. Not to mention a weird-looking girl with a lump on her back.

"I'm so very sorry Miranda and Max Fetherlite, my rudeness was an inexcusable lapse. The briefing notes gave me so little background."

"Don't get upset, Elisha Drinkale," said Max, "I know you believe that all sentients should be treated with the respect they are entitled to, given full equality under the law. Perhaps you would like to come with me to meet our foster son Goodboy, who is up a tree in the garden watching for incoming space vessels. Or would you rather stay for tea and cake?"

Chapter Two

Miranda brewed a large pot of fumitory and bugle tea, and as soon as she unlocked the cake tin the smell enticed the twins, Fairy-Mae and Goodboy into the kitchen. Later, Elisha Drinkale was sitting on a large sofa in the playroom, holding her plate containing an enormous slice of caraway seed cake. She was bookended by Goodboy and Fairy-Mae dribbling over her sleeves, with the twins struggling to get onto her knee and licking the plate edge.

Eventually Miranda felt Elisha had been punished enough, and gave the children their own special cupcakes made with a large spoonful of syrup of poppy seeds, papaver somniferum. Afterwards the children nodded off, and Max carefully lifted them off Elisha's knee, and onto their own sofa.

"We find the peace and quiet cake the most effective way to administer their prescribed calming medication," commented Max, "It is designed to reduce aggressive behaviour to each other as well as ourselves."

Whilst the children slept, Miranda and Max gave Elisha Drinkale a briefing on their foster children and their issues. Firstly, Miranda showed a picture of two tall adult humanoids on her commscreen – one slender with light-blue skin and the other chunky with a bright orange skin, the parents of the twins. Explaining that the twins had been born during their business visit last year.

When the parents left the babies were too small to take with them, accordingly the twins were given to Miranda and Max to foster. On their parents return in two or three long cycles, the twins should have reached their permanent gender. Overtly cheery and pleasant natured, the twins liked to dig for worms and beetles in the garden and sometimes munched the plants, but because they also liked taking small bites out of their foster parents and siblings, meant they were avoided where possible.

"Goodboy sounds a strange name-for the boy," commented Elisha, "holding her plate out for more tea and cake."

Miranda explained that Goodboy had been a feral child found living with a tribe of wild canines by a Forest Warden four years ago, and at that time spoke only in grunts and sidled like a crab on all fours. The warden and his wife had started looking after the boy, and said 'Good Boy' to him when he learned new, 'more human' behaviours. This led to the child thinking 'Goodboy' was his name. However, he wasn't good at all. The warden bought Goodboy boots to help him walk upright, and he did learn how to stand up, but also to kick. Especially when it was time for a shower or tooth cleaning.

Max and Miranda showed their battered and bruised shins, but explained that if they removed the boots he started his sideways scuttle again. When Goodboy wasn't sleeping or eating he liked to climb up to his tree vantage point in the garden, and they tended to leave him there.

"I remember that Leslee's notes said that Fairy-Mae (such a pretty name!) is growing quickly, which causes some kind of problem?"

Miranda explained that Fairy-Mae belonged to an unusual hybrid species of human – Homo Lepidopseris. In order to grow quickly Fairy-Mae needed to moult her skin every cycle or so. This 'ecdysis' was an important ritual for Fairy-Mae and she stuck each of her 'sheds' around the wall of her room, giving it a rather sinister look, not to mention creating an unpleasant crackly carpet of skin cells when they dried out.

"And I noticed a lump on her back. Is that a problem for her?" asked Elisha.

"We are told that it's a wing bud. On her final moult the wings will open out, and in her adult state she will have no teeth and feed on liquids, they say. That is, until her teeth grow back after she has mated. Her unlucky mate will only get a limited respite, as she likes to bite if things don't suit her. Max tends to look after her – though her teeth still make dents on his arms." Max demonstrated.

43

"What will happen then? When she gets her wings?" asked a fascinated Elisha, "Will she fly away?"

"Hope not! We are told her parents will come and whisk her off to get married as soon as her final moult starts,". said Miranda, "which we hope is going to be fairly soon as Max is particularly busy with new arrivals in our bonded warehouse."

"I noticed that building as I came in. I think Leslee mentioned that you looked after things for ongoing transit to other planets for short periods of time."

"We keep all kinds of living organisms for up to two full cycles in temperature- controlled conditions. Some cold, like seeds and eggs, some frozen like rare cetacean embryos. Max has to constantly monitor the temperatures. We can't have the giant Venusian cockroaches hatching can we? ...."

As they awakened, Goodboy put his arm around Fairy-Mae and nuzzled her neck. She turned round and bit him, showing her long pointed teeth.

"Get off me you disgusting hairy, smelly animal!" she shouted.

The twins joined in the resulting melee, and Max lifted up both children, one under each arm, and disappeared with the wriggling, swearing bodies through the door and up the stairs, followed by the excited twins.

"Max will put them into their rooms to quieten down," explained Miranda, "They are all nearing puberty and this is happening more and more."

"It must be very stressful," said Elisha.

"Well, we were hoping you were coming to tell us that you have found another foster carer for Goodboy," said Miranda, " especially as Max is so busy at the moment."

"No," said Elisha with a guilty look.

"In that case, let me get us both a glass of my home-made pumpkin and blackberry wine. Then you can tell me what you have come for."

Elisha opted to have a pennyroyal cordial instead, but Miranda poured herself a large glass of wine, took a slurp and then filled the glass up again. Then she sat back.

"OK!" she said, "Let me guess, you want us to take another impossible to place foster child." Miranda took another slug of her wine. "Or equally horrendous, look after another load of eggs to incubate. If you remember, we nearly landed in prison when the last lot got eaten. 'Miranda and Max Fetherlite, you are charged with multiple counts of culpable eggslaughter, for which the prescribed punishment is 15 years hard labour' the judge said. It's already a nightmare having foster children we have to keep locking up instead of spending time with them doing creative and educational things. How would you like to try baking or cooking with foster children trying to eat all the ingredients and dripping saliva into the pans? Max has to stand next to me so they can nip him instead of me. You'd better ask me what you came to ask, but the answer will probably be no!"

The shouting and banging noise upstairs had been replaced by an ominous silence, but neither of them noticed.

Elisha looked very uncomfortable. "I'm sorry you feel so tired and stressed Miranda. but I don't think that the foster child we are hoping you will care for will be hard to look after, and he certainly doesn't bite. You wouldn't notice him. In fact, you haven't noticed him at all, because he came into your house with me, and he is here in this room now!"

"What trick are you playing now?" asked Miranda, slurping the last mouthful of her wine.

"Maybe you'd like me to get you some more wine?" said a quiet, pleasant voice.

Miranda looked to where the voice came from and saw a boy, perhaps 12 or 14, dark-skinned with a shock of red hair and dressed in a smart shirt and tie and trousers with a sharp crease. He looked like pictures of boys from a long ago century.

"I'm Albert, named after Albert Einstein because I'm so clever," he said, smiling at Miranda.

The smile nearly did it on its own, helped by the wine. Quiet AND smiling. Wow! What a role model for the others!

Miranda held out her glass. "Just a smidgeon," she said.

"Perhaps I could get myself a tiny piece of that lovely cake, and a little pennyroyal cordial whilst I get your drink?" Albert asked. Miranda waved her arm to give permission.

"Go on, tell me," said Miranda to Elisha, "What's the snag with this one? And where was he hiding?"

"This is the snag," said Albert.

Miranda turned to look at him, but he wasn't there. Gone.

"Albert's father is a time scientist and whilst Albert was helping him with the research into other dimensions (no I don't know what that is either) the flask holding the product exploded and Albert was sprayed with the liquid. Ever since then he keeps disappearing to somewhere else." explained Elisha.

"Most times I can stop myself appearing, but can't really control when I disappear," explained Albert, "Which is why I need to stay with someone who can keep this a secret."

"What about your mother and father?" asked Miranda.

"Both recovering in hospital," answered Elisha, "But Albert needs a home for some time."

"Everything seems very quiet upstairs," said Albert, "Are you sure everything is alright?"

Just then, there was an almighty crash, and they heard a clumping down the stairs, then something fell against the door at the bottom of the stairs.

Albert quickly ran to the door, followed by a wobbly Miranda. When he opened it Max's head rolled into the room. Miranda screamed and screamed.

Chapter Three

Senior Security Investigator Inspector Hermann Steinbeck, accompanied by his colleague, Security Investigator Sergeant Walt Hemingway, came within the 27 minutes stipulated for arrival at murder scenes. Elisha Drinkale met them at the door and briefed them quickly on the special nature of the house inhabitants.

"I'm the Foster Family Liaison person, and I was here to check on these special foster children and their remarkable foster carers. I do not have to remind you that all sentients are accorded equal rights to police investigation and protection. Miranda Fetherlite is in no state to talk to you - she is distraught by the death of her partner, Max. I will try to help you as well as I can."

Elisha took them through the playroom and past a loudly sobbing Miranda, and showed them the body of Max and its detached head at the bottom of the stairs.

"But this is an android," said Sergeant Hemingway, "Can't it be mended?"

Miranda shrieked, "If your head came off, could you be mended?"

Something nudged Elisha in the ribs. "I just need to get a drink for Miranda," said Elisha.

Albert whispered to Elisha whilst she poured Miranda some pennyroyal cordial.

"Inspector, I think the issue is that, even if Max could, as you suggest, have that head, or another one, put onto the body, the result would not be Max, but a stranger. This is clearly a murder case. And I will be contacting the media to report it if there is any delay in the investigation." said Elisha with a flourish, handing Miranda her cordial.

After tasting Miranda handed it back, "A glass of wine, please. A large one. And, Elisha, thank you for your understanding and support. Tell me where has thingy gone? The one we can't see?"

"All children are in their rooms. Miranda," said Elisha, pointedly, hoping she would keep quiet about Albert in front of the Security Investigators.

To the Inspector she said, "We'll want to keep Max's body here with us. Won't we, Miranda?" Miranda nodded. "Perhaps you could move Max into the sitting room, please."

"Of course, Miranda Fetherlite," said the Inspector, "Then can we take some statements."

Miranda gave Elisha the code for unlocking the children's bedroom doors and she went up and unlocked them one by one, and told them what had happened. They were quiet and subdued, and Elisha told the children that they needed to tell the investigators anything they remembered. They trooped downstairs. Their stories were very similar.

"Max took me to my room and came in to tell me off for swearing and kicking, he said I could have supper if I was good," said Goodboy

"Max took me to my room and said I shouldn't bite and swear, and I had to change out of Miranda's wedding dress and hang it up. He said I could have supper if I was good," said Fairy-Mae.

The twins just said, "He locked us in and said we could come out later."

Then they all agreed that after that everything went quiet. Later they heard talking. Then there was a thump and a crash.

Miranda and Elisha said that they had heard nothing until the thump of Max falling or being pushed down the stairs.

Inspector Steinbeck gave his men instructions to search the house and large garden and check outside the grounds to see if there were places for outsiders to enter the house. A rash of constables appeared and started randomly searching (though why they needed to look in the cake tin, Elisha had no idea).

Elisha helped Miranda into bed and gave her a peace and quiet cupcake and some pennyroyal tea, which she meekly drank.

Elisha commed Leslee Streetfighter and told her of the tragic happenings. "What about Albert?" Leslee asked. "He is here, and I hope he can help us," said Elisha.

"Are you here Albert?" asked Elisha. No reply. Elisha felt quite panicky, she had been hoping Albert would have an idea what to do. Going into the kitchen to see what there could be for the children's suppers, she found a bowl and a spoonful of cereal disappearing out of it into nothing.

"Are you there Albert?" she asked.

Albert appeared with milk and cereal spilled down his nice shirt.

"How did that happen?" asked Elisha.

"When I disappear I go several seconds into the future and it's difficult to co-ordinate eating. Can you keep a look out whilst I finish?"

Elisha stood at the window and watched the constables walking in and out of the bushes in the garden. One was even climbing Goodboy's tree. Two forensic technicians dressed in their white suits and bootees came into the playroom. One went up the stairs and one went into the sitting room.

Albert, who now was hiding in the larder was obviously starving, and he had a second helping of food. Elisha looked on the shelf in the larder and found bread and cheese labelled 'children's suppers', as well as something for herself.

"What can we do to help find Max's murderer?" she asked.

"I've got plenty of ideas," replied Albert, "For now I'm going into the sitting room to watch the Forensic Officer with Max. He disappeared."

Later Inspector Steinbeck and Sergeant Hemingway came in to report to Miranda, though as she was sleeping spoke to Elisha instead.

"You can tell Miranda Fetherlite that we have found no

evidence of someone being able to enter from outside the property – the security systems are substantial. It isn't even possible for someone outside the fences to see into the garden and the force field over the property would have disabled any drone. This supports the idea of the murderer of Max Fetherlite being already in the house, or hiding in the warehouse somewhere. We will continue tomorrow when the forensic team will have their report."

Elisha gave the children their supper and afterwards they chose to go back in their own rooms to watch PicFlix. She left some food for Albert in the sitting room, but he didn't answer when she spoke. Finally, she checked on the deeply sleeping Miranda, leaving her a flask of fumitory and bugle tea, then found a spare bedroom to sleep in.

Chapter Four

Elisha woke up at 5 o'clock and found herself fully dressed in her crumpled clothes and went to the bathroom to freshen up before another stressful day started. She tried talking to Albert in several rooms, but if was there, he didn't reply. Miranda was still fast asleep, snoring gently, so Elisha left her for a while.

Elisha knocked on the twin's door. There was a scrabbling and snuffle against the door.

"What?"

"This is Elisha, remember, I saw you yesterday. I was wondering if you wanted to come into the bathroom for a shower or a wash before breakfast?"

"No. No washing, no teeth brushing, we're not dirty."

She had the same reaction at Fairy-Mae's and Goodboy's door. She tried again.

"Do you want to come down for breakfast?" Inevitably, this worked. Once she opened their doors, Elisha was knocked over in the rush.

"What do you eat for breakfast?" she asked.

Fairy-Mae opened a cupboard and there, on the shelves, were bottles and boxes labelled 'Twins', 'Goodboy', 'Fairy', 'Miranda/Visitors'.

"Breakfast cupboard," Fairy-Mae said, and then went on to dilute the blackcurrant and betaney cordial to make a breakfast drink for them.

Elisha left the children helping themselves to their food, and went to wake Miranda with a mint tea, and some of her cereal on a tray. And an aspirin.

Miranda was much the worse for wear after yesterday's bottle and a half of wine, but the hangover did distract her from starting crying about Max. Whilst Miranda drank her tea, Elisha told her what the Security Investigator had said.

"They'll be coming today to report to you," said Elisha, "But I'll have to go home to get changed. Do you want me to come back to help?"

"You are so kind," said Miranda, "and I'll be very grateful if you can stay for a day or two. By the way, where is that boy you brought with you? The one who disappears?"

"Albert," answered Elisha, "As the police were all over the house yesterday, he thought he could be more help if he stayed out of the way and watched things for us. Last I saw of him he was in the sitting room with Max."

Miranda looked at her breakfast and had a thought, "Elisha, how much breakfast did you give to the children?"

"I didn't give it to them, they helped themselves," she answered.

"OMG they'll kill themselves!" Saying that Miranda jumped out of bed and ran downstairs.

The kitchen was empty. Breakfast plates were empty. Jars of food were almost empty-the fact there was food left wasn't for lack of trying. The children were on the sofa in the playroom, groaning.

"Don't be mad with Elisha – that was a brilliant breakfast. The first time I have been trusted to help myself." said Goodboy.

"And the last!" said Miranda, "No food for all of you for two days!"

Whilst the children settled down to sleep off their breakfast in the playroom, Miranda went up to get dressed before the Security Investigators returned, and Elisha went home for a change of clothes.

Everything was quiet for a while, but something was happening in the sitting room.

After a shower and a change of clothes Miranda went down to spend time with Max before the Special Investigators returned. She opened the sitting room door quietly taking a deep breath to prepare herself. As she peeped around the door, she started to scream. Albert was messing with Max's head; she saw that there were wires going from Max's digicomp into the android's head.

Miranda stormed over to him, "Take your hands off my Max! I will have you arrested for interfering with evidence for the investigation into his murder!"

"Miranda, my darling. Please don't be angry." said Max's voice coming from its head, "Albert says he will help us."

"Max! Max!" Miranda stroked Max's face, "Oh my dear," she said, "I thought I'd lost you for ever."

After a little while Miranda looked at Albert. "How did you know how to do this?" she asked.

"I'm really good with electronics but it took me most of the night to work out the wiring and to check that Max's brain hadn't been harmed." Albert answered.

"My darling," Miranda asked Max, "Can you tell us what happened to you? Who did this?"

"I don't know," replied Max, "All I remember is being hit on the back of the head."

"Did you lock the children in their rooms?" asked Miranda.

"I can't remember," said Max. "Albert has told me about his condition, and I agree with him that he might help us find my attacker if he stays invisible."

"How do we stop the Inspector finding out about you now?" Miranda asked Max.

"I think we should cover Max up with that big curtain, and you can tell the police that you don't want his body touched. I'm sure they will respect your wishes," said Albert, "and you can come in and tell Max what is happening when there is nobody around."

"What about Elisha Drinkale?" asked Miranda.

"I think she should stay if you need her to help you for a

little time, but it's better if you don't mention me mending Max." Albert then disappeared.

Miranda stayed a while chatting, then covered up Max and then went and shut the room door behind her.

Suddenly there was screaming, and Miranda ran as quickly as she could into the playroom.

There was Goodboy, doubled over and shouting with pain, and Fairy-Mae shouting, "Help him, Help him!"

Miranda went to the cupboard and got out a jar containing white powder, she put some into a cup, added water and stirred it, all the time keeping calm. She had been here before.

"Come on, Goodboy, drink this. I told you eating too much breakfast would make you sick."

And he was, very. As Miranda cleaned him up, she tried to help him drink some of the stomach medication. Good boy began to sweat and have trouble breathing, and bent over with more stomach cramps. Then he went quiet.

The Security Investigators arrived with a Forensic Technician just as Miranda was about to ring the doctor for advice. She shouted to them that Goodboy was ill and she was about to ring the doctor. When they got back into the playroom Goodboy had gone quiet. The Forensic Technician leaned over him.

"This child is dead." she said.

"What happened?" asked the Inspector.

Miranda explained about the overeating, showing the empty jar meant for a week's breakfasts.

"I blame myself," said Miranda, "I should have been here!"

The forensic technician put some of the Goodboy's vomit into an evidence bag.

"In an unexplained death after eating, we always need to

check. It's routine," said the Inspector.

The Twins and Fairy-Mae were subdued. Miranda suggested the twins went out to play in the garden and Fairy-Mae opted to go back in her room.

Goodboy was being carried out in a body bag when Elisha arrived. After Miranda explained what had happened Elisha cried because it was 'all her fault'. Miranda said that it was her fault as well, so they both sat down and had a small sorrel brandy.

Two deaths in the family.

Chapter Five

The next time Miranda saw Inspector Steinbeck she knew two things straight away. Firstly, he had some news for them and secondly, it wasn't good.

"Have you some information for us, Inspector?" asked Miranda.

"I'm sorry to have to tell you Miranda (can I call you Miranda?) but analysis of evidence has shown that your foster son, Goodboy, was poisoned with hemlock and your partner was given a heavy blow to the back of the head, so his fall down the stairs was deliberate. As a matter of urgency we need to speak again to everyone who was in the house yesterday."

"That was myself and Elisha Drinkale, and my foster children Fairy-Mae and The Twins. (Miranda did not feel she had to mention Albert, as he had been in the room with them when Max was knocked downstairs but she did feel she had to come clean about something else). But Inspector, I must tell you that I am a qualified herbalist and prescribe herbal medicines for people. I grow hemlock in my garden. I use an infusion for asthma and chest complaints. I also grow other herbs and plants that could be harmful in large quantities."

"If Elisha Drinkale could go and get Fairy-Mae and the Twins, perhaps, Miranda, you can show me where you grow and store your herbs."

Later Inspector Steinbeck sat down in the playroom to talk to the Twins

"Can you tell me in what order were you children locked in your rooms?" he asked Twin One

"Goodboy first, then Fairy-Mae and then us," Twin One said.

"You all told me before that you heard voices after the door was shut. Who was talking?" asked the Inspector.

"One was Max and we thought he was talking to Goodboy, so he must have returned to his room." said Twin One.

"But there are secrets we should tell you before Fairy-Mae does - -though we didn't hurt Max and Goodboy. You see we can get out of our rooms when they have been locked." said Twin Two

The Twins went on to tell the Inspector that they had found a way to climb out of their room through a tunnel they had chewed under the floor and how they would unlock the doors of the other children if they wanted to come out. Sometimes they did, often they didn't because they would rather watch vidds. But they did say that they had all stayed in their rooms the night before. The Inspector was bemused.

"But you're not tall enough to unlock the doors," suggested the Inspector.

The twins laughed and stood up straight. Immediately it was clear that they were more than tall enough. With their long arms they could easily reach to the keypad.

"Do you know what hemlock is?" asked the Inspector.

"My twin is an expert in herbs," said Twin One, "Miranda says we like worms but we also like plants."

Twin Two swelled with pride telling about his knowledge of herbs in Miranda's garden. He had started looking them up on his databox after he tried nibbling the leaves and found that one or two gave him stomach ache. He made a list of ones to avoid – and had told Fairy-Mae and Goodboy about them. Good boy, it seems, used to live in the woods somewhere and he liked to eat herbs – but Twin Two never saw Fairy-Mae eating plants in the garden.

"Do you know which plants are poisonous in Miranda's garden?" asked the Inspector.

"Hemlock, of course, but also foxglove and monkshood – but those two are more garden flowers than herbs. I think deadly nightshade is probably the most dangerous, but there are no berries until autumn, and you'd be silly to eat rhubarb leaves like

I did. I'm practising to be a scientist so I need to experiment!" said Twin Two, "My twin only does things I try first."

"Tell me how I got this itchy rash, then?" said Twin One.

The Inspector was stunned. "Did you know about this?" the inspector asked Miranda, "About the twins studying your herbs and eating them?"

"No, I certainly didn't," said Miranda, "Just wait a minute whilst I get some ointment for that itchy rash."

She returned with a jar of chickweed and calendula ointment, and proceeded to rub it into the tum of Twin One whilst it wriggled and giggled. The Twins then went off back into their room.

Later Inspector spoke to Fairy-Mae and she corroborated the twin's account. The twins would regularly ask if she wanted her door unlocking, but she rarely did, preferring to watch PicFlix. She also heard Max speaking, and at the time she thought the other voice was Goodboy's, but she could think of no reason why Max would go back to talk to him. Like the Twins, she went back upstairs to her room.

"Are you any nearer finding out who played these wicked tricks?" said Miranda.

"No," answered Inspector Steinbeck, "but we have found the vase from the bathroom that was used to hit Max. We also think it was possible that the body was left at the top of the stairs and eventually toppled down causing the crash."

"Thank you for telling me, Inspector," said Miranda, thinking that the murderer or murderers could be the foster children (surely not?) or the elusive Albert, and she knew who she was putting her money on."

"Oh! Inspector," said Miranda, calling after him, "I have some errands to do. When Elisha Drinkale returns, will you tell her to wait and make herself a cup of tea?"

Several hours later, Miranda bustled into the kitchen where Elisha was on her third cup of tea. "I've had to check the temperature in the bond warehouse and rotate some of the crates. A freighter is arriving within the next few days to collect and drop off. After that I went to the hospital to check on Albert's parents. Both are still in a coma, but neither of them, strangely, keep disappearing. Which reminds me, Elisha, have you seen Albert recently?"

"No, Miranda, I thought he would be staying out of the way of the Security Inspectors, and I tried the door to the sitting room, but it's locked."

"Yes, well, I needed to keep Max and my time together private, said Miranda.

A few minutes and a small brandy later, they heard shrieks from the Twins.

"What now?" said Miranda, quite worn out with all the drama.

Security Sergeant Hemingway had heard and came running in and set off up the stairs, followed more slowly by Miranda and Elisha. They found both Twins in their room writhing about, trying to pick very large biting red ants off their bodies. As an ant ran up the Sergeant's trouser legs and several ran over Elisha's shoes, even louder shrieks were added to those of the Twins.

Just then, a shiny silver figure holding a container, streaked past them into the room, grabbed hold of the twins, carried them into the bathroom, and put them under the shower. Simultaneously sluicing the Twins with one hand and picking up the ants and putting them through a funnel into the container with the other. Max, for yes, this is who it was, began to take charge of the situation. Max picked the final ants off the Sergeant's leg, and chased those climbing over Elisha's feet. Miranda, who knew what they were, had stayed well out of range. Max tracked down every last one of the incredibly valuable Giant Bellotian Fire Ants that had been inside sealed boxes in the bonded warehouse for onward transport to the Interplanetary Zoological Space Station. Mind you, there were one or two that had been squashed under foot, and one or two eaten by the Twins, but that was not a mistake they would make again. Serves them right, thought Miranda for opening the mysterious box left under a bed in their room.

The Sergeant's leg swelled up like a balloon, and with the leg, and the Twins, sprayed with calamine and wrapped in wet towels, the three of them were rushed off to hospital with severe bites and burns. Given the relatively small size of the Twins bodies they could die

One death in the family, a resurrection and two more family lives threatened.

Chapter Six

Miranda was frustrated, things were never sorted out to her satisfaction. Inspector Herman Steinbeck was as clueless about what had happened at the end as he was at the beginning. There was no denouement, as she knew was supposed to happen. Dramas always had the detective revealing the names of the culprits at the end. But given that no one had actually told him the truth it was impossible for him to even speculate.

The Inspector had really annoyed her when he said, "It's nice to see Max mended and looking very smart and shiny!"

Miranda's response was withering, "Anyone can see this is not Max, you fool. I claimed on my insurance and this is MarkTwo - a replacement android, which, even though they downloaded data, it didn't re-create my partner. It is taking over managing the bond warehouse, but we will no longer look after Foster Children."

At night Miranda lay down in bed with Max's head next to her on its pillow, attached to his reactor powerpack. They had talked at length over what could have happened but as Albert had probably removed key memories about his attack, Max could only speculate.

"If I hadn't actually locked his door then it could have been Goodboy; but it could also have been Albert, who had hit me and then somehow propped me up to fall later. Or I suppose I could have tripped up and fallen."

"Rubbish! Not an accident!" said Miranda, "The children heard you talking to someone. It had to be Albert who hit you AND poisoned Goodboy AND stole the Fire Ants from the warehouse."

"Where do you think Albert has got to?" asked Max.

"He has made himself scarce. The police can't find an invisible boy can they? That reminds me, Elisha Drinkale has disappeared as well. I thought she was my friend."

Miranda was reasonably happy how things had worked out. Every night she could come to bed and talk through the day's events, and have Max tell her she is beautiful. If Max started to hum, she could always switch him off to let him cool down.

Elisha Drinkale gave up her job as Foster Family Liaison. She gave her notice in to Leslee Streefighter.

"Post Traumatic Stress." she said.

Actually, she felt very guilty after failing to tell Miranda that she had seen Albert heading into the Bond Warehouse before the ants were left in the Twins' room. She was complicit in the injuries to the Twins but hadn't seen him at all after that, and was now wondering what had happened to him. After waiting around a day or two, she bought a ticket to Tunnel City on Ceres, to keep out of sight for a while.

Fairy-Mae saw the separation cracks appearing on the side of her head and knew the final moult was beginning. Her parents' FTL Space Freighter was due to be in orbit tomorrow and the landing craft would pick her up within 24 hours.

Before it was time to go, she went to visit the Twins in hospital. Even though they were still very swollen and blotchy it was clear from what could be seen under the dressings that both of them were changing skin tone to the same colour, from the bright green towards a pale blue, and it looked like they had doubled their height.

"Well, congratulations girls!" said Fairy-Mae. "You are so grown up! What are you going to call yourselves?"

"I'm Fairy," said Twin One, "And she's Mae. "

"Our parents are on the way-we'll be home within a cycle. Miranda has already said Good Bye to us," added Twin Two.

Flattered by their choice of names Fairy-Mae was partially reassured. Whilst she chatted Fairy-Mae scanned their faces for any clue they knew what she had done. There was no sign. She thought it was pretty obvious she hated living with Miranda and

Max. She hated them, especially Max. And she particularly hated Goodboy and the way he nuzzled her neck and pawed her.

That night when they had been fighting and carried ignominiously upstairs, she just snapped and whacked Max across the head with the vase whilst it was talking to Goodboy. Goodboy had delivered a kick at Max when it was on the floor, and the head came off. So, in fact, they were both involved. The Twins had already gone into their room, so perhaps they really didn't see either of them do it.

Of course, Goodboy had to be dealt with, and because he was so greedy that was easy. After that there was the weird scene when Fairy Mae had heard Elisha Drinkale talking to herself in the kitchen about 'staying invisible', 'keeping out of the way of the Investigators' and 'hide in the warehouse Albert'.

She understood what was happening when she saw a boy appear coming out of the larder. Waiting in the garden outside the warehouse Fairy-Mae saw the boy appear out of nowhere again and head off to the warehouse. She followed him inside and had shouted 'Albert! I need help'. And lo and behold the boy fell into the trap and popped up in front of her. Another whack with the stone she brought with her and Albert dropped onto the floor.

Frightened he might disappear if she left him too long, Fairy-Mae peeped into several crates in the refrigerated section and found one a quarter full of small boxes, and labelled 'Soundproofed Crate for Bellotian Fire Ants in Transit. Add Padding to Prevent Breakage'. Fairy-Mae had picked up Albert, staggered over to the crate and. tipped him in. It was fate! She knew the ants were there for a purpose, and took a box back to give a little surprise for the Twins. After that she then had a blissful two weeks of solitude during which she bonded with Miranda and they became friends.

Fairy-Maw now saw nothing in the Twin's behaviour that revealed any hiding of guilty knowledge. Though she had come to the hospital ready for terminating her relationship with the Twins, drastic action was not needed.

After she had gone, one of the Twins got up and watched her go down the corridor and out through the swing doors.

"She's gone! Do you think we fooled her?"

"Quick thinking! That bit about 'Fairy' and 'Mae' convinced her. I could see she was going to get rid of us if she thought we knew she killed Goodboy."

Sometime later Miranda was in bed bringing Max up to date with all the news.

"Here's a holo of the twins, Hyacinth and Sapphire with their parents in their new home, and a vid of Fairy-Mae wearing my wedding dress – I bet she tore it fitting it round those wings which were actually smaller than I expected. And the landing craft arrived for the refrigerated cargo which reminds me that MarkTwo told me that when he returned the Fire Ants to their crate there seemed to be piles of padding left over on the floor as though something extra was in the crate."

"That sounds to me as if somebody could have put the missing Albert in there," said Max. "Nobody here could hear him scream two minutes in the future."

"Not our problem and it serves him right anyway for what he did to you and Goodboy."

"I'm not convinced he hurt either of us," said Max. "And remember he did save me so I can talk to you now."

"Ah, Well! There is that." said Miranda grumpily. It made her very angry when Max disagreed with her. She remembered with a smile how MarkTwo had told her yesterday how nice she looked in the new dress.

Putting down her wine glass Miranda leaned over Max and unplugged him.

The Beatification of Android Annie

Chapter One

Egdar unscrewed the top of the packing case and checked over the android whilst carefully removing its protective sealant. Its face, a perfect, almost human mask, protected the sophisticated nanoelectronics underneath. The custom-made lightweight body was built for strength: fabricated from cerium-erbium modified titanium alloy with inner parts a smorgasbord of artificial elastomers, woven cellulose and muscle tissue with grown-on ultra-fast nerves. Specialised multi-tool hands covered with an electroplated film of beryllium-copper bronze completed this distinctive hominoid. More than half of Egdar's loan was spent on this 'genius' android so he could offer unique services to this growing community. Egdar had been, up until now, unable to open up a market for using the android's talents (though he was not sure exactly what they were – the neuroprocessor's handbook was pretty vague). But it was time for it to pay for itself. Edgar needed to earn enough money to provide exit velocity from this place.

Egdar Bester, sole proprietor of 'Bester's Robots – Home of Household Robots and Specialised Androids' – wondered (and not for the first time) how he had managed to fall for the blurb in the glossy brochure but still came to the same conclusion. There were no actual lies.

"Get away from it all" – well, he had known that Toraxx 9 was pretty well the back yard of the Toraxx system, but it wasn't so much the back of beyond as turn left at the end of the rainbow and get lost.

"Toraxx 9 has a temperate climate, oxygen atmosphere and plenty of water – stand on the balcony of your own architect-designed stilt-house and workshop, built on your own island, and look out on the verdant landscape. With a growing population this is just the place to set up your business."

Egdar stood on his balcony with its ultra-thick window and looked out at the swamp. Green swamp as far as the eye could see. As he watched, he saw a massive bubble of swamp gas reach the surface, and belch its contents into the air. Several eructations later a huge brown cloud was left hanging above the water, and his window splattered with unmentionable wriggly things.

Indeed, the air was oxygen-rich and breathable but the disgusting smell permeated everything. There had been no mention of that, or of the fact that it was hardly possible to pay off the loan in 10 years. Or indeed, if you weren't already a swamp-food vegan you soon would be. There were limits to the extent your syntho-cook could rehash the no doubt healthy swamp protein.

The currently occupied tropical zone of Toraxx 9 consisted of continuous swamp. Every so often prolific bog vegetation created large tangled clots floating on the underlying marshland. These became, over time, small islands strong enough to carry sealed houses built on stilts with filtered air and water. Almost the whole of the immigrant ten-year indentured population lived in separate households on little islands. Most of them worked long hours in the massive swamp vegetation processing plant to pay off their debt, but had so little extra time they clubbed together to hire Egdar's household driver-cum-cook robots. He also did quite well with his mechanica-robots programmed to mend the little skimboats all the poorer population used to travel between islands. But his income still wasn't high enough to save anything. Egdar was 34 and he was pretending he didn't see the first grey hairs in his black hair. He had no more time to waste.

Egdar checked over the special android he had been reluctant to expose to the Toraxx 9 corrosive atmosphere. He lifted the android and its data pods out of the packing case and laid them on his bench. The android already had phenomenal processing power but even so, Egdar used the pods to update its already encyclopaedic knowledge with more medical and scientific information, along with background to the Toraxx planets.

He then worked on the android's sensory receptive

structures, extending the multi-bandwidth sensors in eyes and hands. Finally, he checked all flexible joints were fully sealed before fitting biosynthoskin over the whole body - using xylem cells grown onto gold-vanadium mesh. He tested all networks, inserted the sealed hydrogen reactor, waited for systems controls to show green and then switched it on. Eyes opened. Then closed again.

"Are you alright?" asked Egdar.

"I'm thinking-'Cogito ergo sum'," replied the android in a pleasant, modulated tone. (Egdar looked it up 'I think therefore I am' so what was that about?)

Egdar waited a bit. "What are you thinking about?" he asked.

"I'm wondering why you have crammed all this random data into my brain. What do you think you are preparing me for?" It replied.

"I want you to do more sensitive and complicated work than my other robots," explained Egdar, "and earn enough money to charter a ship off this planet."

"Well, you could have started with giving some background to this planet instead of loading data on 'Polite Phrases and Idiomatic Language in Interplanetary Anglic', which, by the way, I am finding absolutely fascinating." said the android.

"I was only trying to prepare you to speak more like a human, and less like a robot," said Egdar. He then went on to describe the general overview of Toraxx 9 and the planet's administration.

He explained to the android that only the largest island had any semblance of firm land under it. It was home to the Space Port and the Administration for what it was (the Planet Manager's Office with four officers and the Police Station with six). But mainly housed the planet's major source of income, the large warehouse and processing factory turning swamp weed into rare metals and protocarb blocks used for islander's food. The factory was also used for the purification of swamp water and the fermenting of swamp beer and production of Toraxx 'Island Gin'. This was already getting quite a reputation in the Toraxx system amongst connoisseurs who obviously didn't know what it was made from. The planet's small hospital and larger prison were each on their own islands, the prison on the second largest island.

After the explanation the android closed its eyes and switched itself off, and Egdar was forced to grapple it off the table and lean it up against the wall. Then, on his view screen, Egdar commed several key people offering them the first chance to have a prodigiously clever multi-skilled, problem- solving android to work in their organisation.

He tried his fellow business people first: Joely the furniture-maker who used compressed swamp weed blocks to make tables and chairs. Aarkus, who ran a Swap Shop, and Zorro the Smith, fashioning Torexx 9 swamp metals into tools. Then Orso and Throop who made clothes with linen-like fabric from swamp grass. Finally, Mimmu who ran a most successful business – the Coffee Shop – with no coffee but gin and swamp-flour cakes. People didn't go for the food but to meet other trapped residents. Mimmu charged five credits for each hour a seat was occupied. But none of Egdar's business contacts wanted a high-spec android. Or rather, they could see openings for such a resource, but had no money to pay for it.

Egdar started vidding key people in Toraxx 9's administration. Unfortunately, the large viewscreen showed everyone he vidded the whole room, so those contacted looked less than impressed when they saw his android propped against the wall looking asleep (as indeed it was). However, a few opportunities were suggested.

The android opened its eyes. "I'm assuming you expect me to do one of these activities?" It said.

"Forget the swamp-grass processor or the swamp-grass cutter," It continued. "Apart from the ignominy of it, my skin would lift off. Also, you can forget the hospital orderly. A neurosurgeon, perhaps, an orderly, no. But I might consider the

Security Guard job at the Space Port if I can have a nice uniform. Besides I might have the chance to find out how to depart from this place."

So, Egdar kitted his android out with uniform and body armour and a helmet it was thrilled with. "I'm calling you Hector," he said.

Hector zipped away in a skimboat to the Space Port then three days later skimmed back again with a large bonus.

The Director of the Space Port confirmed that Hector had been able to review all their procedures and practices, but just as importantly Hector had scared everyone he found trespassing or even just looking suspicious. Hector had gently gripped each person he found by the shoulder and days later a continuing twinge was a constant reminder.   Hector also, as part of its own private review of the security in the Manager's office, extruded a thin rod from its finger, stuck it in the data port of the main computer and downloaded all the Planet's personnel planning and systems data, including the Space Freighter's cargo manifest and passenger lists.

Later a quick sweep of hospital security enabled Hector to hide a substantial stash of pharmaceuticals in the large storage space behind its breastplate and alter the amounts on records. It was clear humans on this planet used huge amounts of these drugs, so Hector felt they might come in useful to have in the future. So much for security.   After three days the Space Port and major buildings were clear of problems and Hector out of work.

Egdar was stuck to find another role for the android as the openings for belligerent polymaths were few and far between. The android seemed quite happy foraging in the swamp, picking swamp plants and spending time in a small workshop. It extracted chemicals from the swamp water and vegetation, dried some plants in bunches and made a number of potions.

But an opening did present itself. A client with two of his top-of-the-range household robots, complained about the robots 'freezing' as the systems crashed through overloading. This was the wife of Planet Manager Redick, whose family lived in a flat next to the Administration building. When Egdar questioned Mrs Redick he realised that things had changed since they updated to two robots. Now, the teenage son of her husband had arrived to live with them, and on the same transport came two large guard dogs which were totally out of control. The son required tutoring. Mrs Redick was too exhausted and stressed to cope with it all.

"I am just at the far end! I am near to breakdown! I need a robot with initiative to take care of things," she sobbed.

Egdar was sympathetic and said he was not surprised, because household robots were not designed for such advanced duties.

"What I suggest you need is a multi-tasking high-calibre android to act as a superior mother's helper: nurse, tutor, dog-trainer, household robot supervisor and general household manager," said Egdar, "but I have to tell you such a sophisticated android does not come cheap."

"I suppose you are offering my services?" said the android, waking up from sleep in the corner.

Egdar craftily tried to appeal to the android's overweening sense of self-importance, "Actually I doubt whether you can actually do this multi-tasking multi-skilled work. Dogs, stressed and depressed mother, tutoring a teenager, managing a household. You probably are not up to it, especially as you can't go as Hector. You would have to look at least a bit gentle and caring. Perhaps...Annie, Android Annie?"

"Would I get to wear a dress?" said the android.

"Perhaps a tunic with tights, and I suppose you would need a wig," replied Egdar, realising what it was that attracted the android.

"Pink dress and blonde wig or I'm not doing it."

Android Annie had to settle for shrink-fit navy synthoprot bodysuit with pink tunic and navy jacket. But it did get a neat blonde wig.

Chapter Two

Android Annie arrived into an atmosphere of total family chaos: the teenage son was poking the frantically barking dogs with a stick, the small room was full with furniture, random stuff and viewscreen, and Mrs Redick was nowhere in sight.

The android took off its back pack and set to work. Tied up the dogs. Forcibly removed the stick from the son. Then it gripped him gently on the shoulder. His eyes glazed and Annie lowered him down into a chair. Then went to track down Mrs Redick, who looked no more than a young girl when Annie found her sobbing in bed. Clearly Mrs Redick was currently unable to function in any capacity.

Android Annie told Mrs Redick, "Don't worry I'll soon have things organised."

Annie waded through piles of possessions in the lounge and tasked one household robot to put it in one of the freight boxes piled outside the Administration building. By then the dogs had stopped barking. In the peaceful interlude Annie gave instructions to the household cook robot for the evening meal.

After assessing the situation, Android Annie devised a risky strategy for creating calm. Annie didn't exactly know how risky this was, well, perhaps it did know but as a very newly awakened android it had no moral guidelines to make judgements. This was just the quickest and most effective thing to do in the circumstances.

Annie opened its breastplate and removed several jars of chemicals: including a strong tranquilizer, a muscle relaxant and anti-anxiety medication, and mixed them using different ratios and different strengths into little phials for experimentation. Then rummaging in the back pack, it found the dried leaves of the swamp plant that smelt like peppermint, and made a mint tea infusion with filtered water. After adding a few drops of one of her stronger medications Annie helped Mrs Redick to sit up so she could drink the mixture, with firm persuasion. Mrs Redick leaned over the side of the bed and lifted up a bottle from its hiding place in a vase.

"This is my medicine," she said.

Annie took the bottle of Toraxx 'Island Gin' and said, "Well, you can have a little drink before dinner if you promise to have a sleep now."

Later when the teenage son, Criss, woke up, his truculent attitude was only slightly modified. Tall and heavy for his age Annie realised that he could be a physical threat – and not just to humans. So Annie agreed to let him use his VR headset as long as he worked on his screen lesson afterwards. (There never was an afterwards.)

Android Annie made up its own recipe for tonic by mixing swamp plant sugars and a little ascorbic acid in water, then extruded a tube from the end of its finger and blew carbon dioxide through the mixture. The tonic and a generous slug of gin was taken in to Mrs Redick who sat up to drink it though she refused to get out of bed. Annie promised her another large gin and tonic if she got up, showered and dressed before dinner.

Annie browsed round the bedroom whilst Mrs Redick showered, and looked at a family holopic. It was of Planet Manager Redick and a woman other than Mrs Redick with a small boy. Mrs Redick saw Annie looking at the holopic. "That's his first wife with Criss," she said, "I don't want to stare at her every day, but he won't move it." she said, bursting into tears and lying down on the bed again.

After the second gin she got dressed, and Annie helped her brush her hair. By this time Mrs Reddick had perked up considerably.

It was late when Planet Manager Redick walked through from his adjoining office. After a rushed meal during which he said nothing to his son or wife, he got up to go back into his office. As an afterthought he turned to his wife as he left the table.

"Glad to see you are out of bed at least."

Mr Redick didn't stop long enough to see Mrs Redick slide sideways off her chair. Annie quickly picked her up and carried her off to bed. The android realised, too late, the steep slippery slope it had started on.

Over the next day or two, Android Annie skirted a fine line between extremely unsafe and absolutely necessary by trying to manage the optimum medication for Mrs Redick, at the same time trying to cut down her alcohol intake. This was so she stayed upright at dinner time, though nobody seemed to notice her wobbling into her food. This was only one of several major problems in the family.

The son, Criss, spent his time when not attached to his VR headset, tormenting the dogs. Annie logged the VR as his Tutor sessions as he was probably learning something however unsavoury. Annie found that if Criss was stopped from poking the dogs, he just moved on to poke the robots instead. One robot was put on Chriss-watch permanently.

The android checked the cargo manifest it had downloaded at the Space Port and found that the dogs had been shipped over cheaply as Space Freight in Freeze-Pac. It was known that live animals shipped in this state lost wodges of brain matter on defrosting and became untrainable. They had already started having seizures. So, who allowed this to happen?

Mrs Redick was in a state of mental and physical collapse. His son Criss appeared to be a psychopath. It seemed Planet Manager Redick did not notice, or even care, that his family was dysfunctional and in terminal freefall.

The android knew it had been set up. It was going to be blamed for the whole mess. It needed help to understand humans. It accessed the space-net and enrolled on the Level One Interplanetary Certificate in Human Psychotherapy, with requirements for 40 hours of Practical Activity and submission of Course Notes. The android quickly found some useful guidance in the first lesson: 'make sure your patients are calm and relaxed and get ready to listen to their problems'. Good. This was a clear direction for action.

Android Annie mixed different phials of the tranquillisers and anti-anxiety medications and trialled different dosages to the whole family over a day or two. There was a little blip when Mrs Redick slept through the whole day (though no-one noticed) but eventually an optimum of calmness and relaxation permeated the whole family.

Then Android Annie started the series of Interviews with Course Notes. Mrs Redick wanted to go home to Forexx 1 and have some new dresses and go dancing. Criss wanted to watch porn vidds and have his own flyer. Mr Manager Redick thought a major investor could solve all his problems, and fiddled with papers whilst Annie talked to him. None of the family members wanted to pay any attention to each other or the dogs.

Five days later the good news was that the 40 hours were completed and Annie received her Level One Psychotherapy Practitioners Certificate (with commendation). But more significantly the android finally made the various connections between the dogs, Criss and the Redicks.

Android Annie's short-term thought processor noticeboard had become clogged with threads of disconnected data stuck there whenever it found ideas seemed worth thinking about in more depth. Even so, it was a floating stray phrase from the 'Anglic Phrase Database' that had triggered the initial alarm- 'Oh what a tangled web we weave when first we practice to deceive'.

That was the clue. A web. Fitting together the disparate fragments of data revealed that in this family there was a very big tangled web - there was a cuckoo in the nest, and a wolf in sheeps' clothing and several red herrings. The problem was, the android didn't know which family members knew about the wolf or the cuckoo. The huge processor that was the android brain grappled with the human dimension.

Android Annie knew something drastic needed to happen as the family couldn't go on in medicated therapy under constant threat of collapse for long. Annie commed Egdar. He was distraught at the thought of his android's profitable job coming to an end.

"If you could just have continued for another two months, I could have afforded to go home," he said.

"Do humans only think about 'me, me, me'?" replied his android. "I need some help here."

Egdar and the android devised a plan.

Chapter Three

It was with considerable naivete that the android planned for what would be its first major Life Crisis. It had totally underestimated the ability of overtly ordinary humans to anticipate and plan far more scheming, unscrupulous and murderous actions than a genius but inexperienced android and an innocent Egdar could devise. The plan was doomed to fail as it started at the bottom, the least of the problems, rather than the top. The android aimed to neutralise the dogs and get Criss into trouble at the same time.

The plan involved cutting down the sedatives of the dogs and Criss and then getting Mrs Redick to agree to a visit to Mimmu's the day after, by suggesting that she could wear a nice new dress and have a gin when she got there.

The morning started as planned. Mr Redick went into his office and locked the door. Mrs Redick disappeared on the flyer to Mimmu's with a robot. Then the dogs were untied. Annie went to stand by the swamp-pool and then whistled for the dogs as it had trained them. Nothing happened for a few seconds. Then they rushed out of the house and Android Annie called out,

"Criss, Criss, come quickly. The dogs are attacking me."

The dogs rushed up to Annie, jumped up snapping at its jacket. Criss ran up and when he got to Annie, the android shot the animals with its finger laser and they fell dead into the water. It was to appear that Criss pushed the dogs into the swamp. So Annie thought, but it couldn't possibly have anticipated that Criss had been waiting for this chance.

Chriss reached the android and pushed it into the swamp.

Chapter Four

The android heard a man's voice speaking.

"The Magistrate's Court of Toraxx 9 is now in session in the cases of the android owned by Mr Egdar Bester and Criss Redick concerning the death of valuable dogs and criminal damage to the android. Mr Bester is your android awake now?"

Egdar replied, "Yes, Sir."

"Mr Bester, as Chair of this court I am asking, you to give your account of what you saw when you visited the house of Planet Manager Redick to undertake routine updates on your android, which I believe the household called Annie."

Egdar told the Court, "I had a communication from my android confirming that, as Mr and Mrs Redick were to be out of their house, it would be a good time for a routine update of my robots and the android without inconveniencing the family. When I got to the house and out of my flyer, I heard the dogs barking. I saw my android next to the swamp with the two dogs jumping up. I heard my android say, 'Criss, Criss, come quickly, the dogs are attacking me.' I saw Criss Redick running from the house, and ran up myself. I saw the dogs falling into the swamp and after that Criss pushed my valuable android into the swamp after them. I saw a thick stick on the edge of the swamp and hit Criss over the head and he fell down. I called the police who took Criss Redick away in handcuffs, and we used a long grapple to drag out my android from the swamp. The police took it away and I didn't see it again until today."

The police officer who arrested Criss Redick and the android confirmed that he had found the scene as Egdar Bester reported and that his story was accurate. Criss Redick had recovered almost immediately and became extremely violent with the officers, seriously injuring one of them. It was necessary to arrest him. Also, the dogs were pulled out of the water, but no injuries could be found. A post-mortem found they had drowned.

Mr Planet Manager Redick spoke only to say the android's owner was paid a substantial fee for it to manage the household and protect the family and the android was responsible for letting the dogs out in the first place.

The Chair of the Magistrates' Court asked Egdar to outline the case for criminal damage against his valuable android.

"The immersion in the caustic swamp water seeped into its joints and has caused the android's bioskin to lift off. Its mobility is severely compromised, and it will cost 800 credits to repair," said Egdar.

"Can your android address the court?" asked the Magistrate.

"Yes, your honour," said the android. "I would like to replay the records I have of Criss Redick and the family dogs." The android then displayed vidds of Criss tormenting the dogs.

The android, with its skin hanging off in strips, and in an unspeakably smelly wig askew, looked a pathetic sight. It spoke, in its pleasant voice, with a burble that might have indicated immersion in swamp water.

"As Mr Redick said, I was responsible for the dogs' care, and even though they were attacking me, I think I should be punished for putting them into danger."

After retiring to consider the case the Magistrates returned with the verdict. Mr Redick to pay 600 credits to Egdar Bester to repair his android on behalf of his son. Criss Redick who was technically a juvenile, to be sent to the high-security section of the prison for an indefinite time for attacking and injuring the police. The android, called 'Annie', when repaired, to be given 100 hours community service based in the prison or other areas under direction of the governor. The Court's decision was declared final and the Court session over.

A Court Officer helped Egdar lift the android onto a trolley and he wheeled it out to the flyer and took him back to the workshop. The android remained obstinately switched off until Egdar began stripping off his bioskin.

"I'd like my new skin to be a kind of darkish beige, with a

little blush on my cheeks. The wig should be a tasteful light brown. Suitable for my new role as Prison Therapist. And I will need a plain dark suit." It told him.

Egdar sighed, "I doubt whether you will be able to practise your therapy, because remember you will be wearing prison uniform until you have finished your community service. I thought you might like to be Hector again"

"Annie will have much wider wardrobe choices, so Hector is out," said the android.

Then Egdar asked. "I'd like to know why you didn't reveal the Redick family secrets for the Court like you planned?"

"I realised that if I'd revealed Criss was a 'Cuckoo in the Nest' because he was not Mr Redick's son at all, Mr Redick could easily have refused to pay you any money for my damage. As it is, you will make a profit, because my joints aren't damaged. You lied about that," said the android.

"Good Point. I didn't think of that. How did you know Criss wasn't his son?"

"The holo of Redick, his first wife and son, clearly showed that his wife and son had blue eyes. Redick has blue eyes. Brown eyes are the dominant gene, so two blue eyed parents don't have a brown eyed son. Criss Redick has brown eyes. Besides which, Redick must have known that this boy was an imposter and has said nothing. Perhaps he bought him like Mrs Redick. I have the financial data that proves Mrs Redick is actually an indentured servant he bought, knowing she had an addiction. I don't want to reveal his lies yet. Planet Manager Redick is planning something for this planet that is dishonest at best and criminal at worst for which he is looking for major investment. This knowledge about his family could come in very useful for bartering should he threaten anyone else," said the android.

"So, are you just going to let him go ahead with these plans?"

"Of course not, I'm going to sleuth during my community service."

"I thought you were going to be Annie the Therapist?" teased Egdar.

"Annie the Therapist-Detective," answered Annie sharply. The android took itself very seriously.

Chapter Five

Little did Annie realise that the prison was the entrance onto its Road to Damascus. Its way to a new life and a war against evil. But first Annie the Android had to learn more about coping with humans.

As soon as Android Annie started its community service in Toraxx 9 prison, it enrolled for the Intermediate Psychotherapy Certificate, and straight away learned new useful techniques. The Course Training vidds demonstrated how, when listening, if the android inclined its head and nodded after each sentence or two whilst leaning forward a little, the most recalcitrant of patients would talk freely to it. The therapist could also put a hand on the patient's arm or shoulder for re-assurance, which was VERY useful to know.

There was a waiting list of prisoners for Annie's cell visits. This involved more hours of listening to human problems that were, to an android, often incomprehensible. In between tales of family breakup, criminal behaviour, and thwarted ambitions, the Android Detective heard very useful fragments of information about Redick's possible plans for the planet. Annie found the data overload of being a therapist-detective clogged up the short-term processor and it needed quiet time to sift through data. It started spending more and more quiet time in the prison chapel sitting down in front of the large cross made of Toraxx 9 special metal alloys.

The Prison Chaplin was assisted in his pastoral duties by two missionary nuns, Sister Olla and Sister Mairy working in this backwater of Toraxx 9 to bring the Christian message to the prisoners. Android Annie watched the nuns in their wonderful habits. And most desperately wanted to be a nun, or rather more superficially, dressed like a nun.

"Can I be a nun?" the android asked the priest.

"You need to have the belief in God and the calling to be a

nun. Start by reading the bible and praying every day for guidance and faith," the priest replied. "You must also pray for help each day to live without sin."

The android had already uploaded the Bible but had failed to analyse what was strangely obscure life guidance, for it turned out that Annie, unwittingly, had been very sinful. Sudden connections in the brain threads revealed to Annie its major issues with the sins of covetousness and envy. Mind you, it took quite a burst of genius to link - 'You shall not covet your neighbour's house. You shall not covet your neighbour's wife, his ox or donkey, or anything that belongs to your neighbour.' – with 'You shall not covet a nun's habit or vidd stars' long curly wigs etc', especially when you can have some things that aren't sins and not others that are.

It also turned out that the Bible was a rich source of phrases the android could use in prisoner- therapy. The prisoners responded well to Android Annie's helpful feedback. To prisoners worried about violence it might say -

"The Bible says 'Do not fear their threats. Do not be frightened' or 'Do not let your heart be troubled, pray to the Lord for help'."

Mind you, the android would also be sure to take a gentle but very firm shoulder grip to bullying prisoners to ensure prayers were answered, working out that it was acting as an instrument of the Lord if they were unconscious for a while. Also, for those who continued to need a little extra help to stop violence a heavy suggestion that they attended church was often taken up.

The priest noticed that Android Annie was the impetus behind a new interest in the church and a considerable decrease in prison violence. Also, Android Annie attended confession every week and the priest was impressed with its growing self-awareness. It did take rather a long time to detail the minutiae of every sinful thought, and the priest learnt more about trivial covetousness than he wished. However, when Annie next asked, "Can I be a nun?" he took it much more seriously.

"Annie," he said, "It is not enough to know the bible. You

have to believe the Word of God in the Bible."

"What if I don't think the miracles were true? What do I do then?" asked Annie.

"You have to pray for faith to let the light of God shine into your life."

Annie continued to visit the prisoners and found time every day to pray in the small chapel. One day a series of loud noises had started to interrupt its pleas for the gift of faith and Annie worried that the Lord might not be able to hear. Looking out of a window Annie saw the noise was a large machine driving piles into the ground and shaking the walls of the church. This was the extension to the prison the plans of which Annie had seen Planet Manager Redick working on at his home office. The current prison building was only about a quarter full so why build an extension unless you've got dishonest ideas? Annie was getting distracted and knew this was the test the Lord was giving it.

The pile-driving vibrations finally dislodged the heavy cross on the wall of the chapel. Focused on the prayer, Annie was unable to prevent the cross falling on its head.

The priest and the two nuns heard the loud crash and rushed into the church. They found Android Annie face down on the floor in front of the altar, pinned down by the cross. Together they lifted off the cross, and the wig fell onto the floor. They could see that the armoured metal of the android's head had only suffered a dinge, but Annie appeared to be damaged. They lifted it into one of the swamp-wood seats.

"I think Annie is broken," said Sister Olla, "We should send for Egdar."

No one said anything else. They sat for a few minutes, and several prisoners joined them and were very upset to see Annie injured. Then the android's eyes opened and a light shone out of one eye.

The android spread its arms and said, "It's a miracle! I prayed for the gift of faith and the Lord answered me! And he sent a sign and I saw a blinding light as faith came into my life."

The android sank to its knees and prayed and was joined by everyone in the church, overawed by the bright light shining out of the android's right eye.

Then the android spoke again, "Through his miracle the Lord has created understanding and clarity out of confusion. I had lost my way and now I'm found."

The word got around the prison and wider into the planet community of the miracle in the chapel, and even though Egdar replaced the damaged component in the android's faulty eye, and the light went out, it only made more special the experience of those who had seen the miracle eye when the android woke up.

It was the task of Sister Olla and Sister Mairy to prepare Android Annie for the formal ceremony to welcome the android into the church. Annie was in a state of pure bliss. First came the habit, draped to the ground, over two underskirts, then a coif over the head with a wimple around the neck and a cape over the chest. Finally, a tunic secured by a belt, the rosary beads and an apron. All made from the wonderful swamp linen by Orso and Throop. The android said 'my cup runneth over' when it finally became Sister Annie. There wasn't a dry eye in the church. Except, of course, Egdar's.

After the ceremony Sister Annie had a quiet word with the Chaplin during confession.

"How do I become a Saint?" the android asked.

The Chaplin knew that the only way to deal with Sister Annie's queries. Honestly and simply as possible. This android, though a valuable member of the church only heard the information it wanted.

"The process starts when the head of the Church says that someone who has died as a martyr or lived a holy life is now in heaven. Then there is consideration of miracles that occurred when people asked for help in the person's name. If this is proved then this is called Beatification. Years and Years later the holy person may be made a Saint. But, Sister Annie, if by some fluke of nature you became Beatified and did become a Saint, you would not know about it, as you would have been dead for many years. And the fact that you asked me this tells me that you are again committing the sin of PRIDE."

The next day Egdar finally managed to get Sister Annie on its own in the dressing room next to the chapel.

"Congratulations," he said, "but your community service is now over and I need you to earn some money urgently. I have to pay my loan."

"Don't worry," said the android. "With the Lord's help I am still working on my plan for the downfall of the villainous Planet Manager Redick and the setting up of the Toraxx 9 Community Collective. At the moment I have found that Redick owns all interplanetary patents using the name 'Toraxx 9' so I want you to register two things under the name of 'Sister Annie'."

The android went to shut the door and then shuffled about to lift up its cape and open the zip on its made-to-measure habit. Sister Annie then opened up the chest compartment (still crammed with jars and bags of plants) and took out two pieces of paper, which it gave to Egdar. The first a recipe for 'Sister Annie's Peppermint Tea Bags made with peppermint planted by Sister Annie', and the second for, 'Sister Annie's Tonic for Gin, a special recipe made with purified water blessed by Sister Annie.'

The android took out the bags of ingredients for the tea bags and tonic and said, "Have Mimmu try them out at the Coffee Shop-and let one of your robots make them up for export. I have sent my ideas for metal containers for the Tonic to Zorro, the Smith. It should be possible to use the offcuts from the metal-rolling mill to process into small bottles."

There was a knock at the door, and before Sister Annie left it said, "Come and meet me at the Planet Manager's Office when the next Space Freighter docks."

As a regal Sister Annie rustled away to her numerous

followers, a stunned Egdar hurried off with the ingredients and instructions because he could see this really working – ideas for marketing and publicity began to pop in to his head. First a news flash to Toraxx SpaceNet of an android becoming Sister Annie after a miracle? Luckily he took a vidd of the ceremony.

Sister Annie's Peppermint Tea was a hit at Mimmu's, almost much as the new Toraxx 9 Gin with Sister Annie's Tonic. Even workers from the processing plant took to dropping after work, possibly due to the rumour spreading like wildfire that Sister Annie's drinks had an antidepressant effect, settled digestive problems due to swamp protein, and many other things depending who you spoke to. More information Egdar used for marketing.

Chapter Six

Sister Annie reckoned that things had to be speeded up if it was going to be a Saint. For a start, there had to be a lot more miracles. People had to be healed. Then Sister Annie needed to be a martyr. First things first. Time in the workshop making careful tinctures and medicines.

Later Sister Annie went fact-finding hospital visiting with Sisters Olla and Mairy and found that many patients were suffering from 'Swamp sickness' and a few from the disfiguring 'Space Fungus'. The day after Sister Annie visited the hospital on its own and stopped by each bed, holding hands briefly. Afterwards, several said that they had felt 'a rush of healing' flow up their arm, another said – 'I felt a sharp prick' and they were all correct. After that there was the ward for patients with 'Space Fungus', an illness where large misshapen growths grew over the face and body. Sister Annie offered them spoonsful of her special tonic and suggested they drank her mint tea.

Within a few days the patients with Swamp sickness all felt better and the Space Fungus had shrivelled up and dropped off. Clearly miracles. Interplanetary News Channels were buzzing as the sheer scale of the healing at Toraxx 9 hospital was revealed. There was a clamour for Sister Annie to visit other planets in the Toraxx 9 system. There were several offers to charter ships to transport her. Sister Annie was focused on completing the mission at Toraxx 9.

During a visit to the Swamp Grass Processing plant Sister Annie told the workers they would soon be free from slavery. And spoke to the prisoners saying how it would intercede with the Lord if they stayed on the right path.

Showdown day came when the Space Freighter arrived. When Planet Manager Redick was busy Sister Annie went with Egdar into Redick's office and spoke over the loudspeaker.

"People of Toraxx 9, this is Sister Annie speaking. I need

your help to overthrow a tyrant. Planet Manager Redick is about to sell this planet to ExoSafeConsortium to use as a Penal Colony. I have seen the plans. He bought a sick girl to act as his wife. He passed an imposter off as his son so he could pretend to have a family and be settled here. All a lie. I ask you to join me here at the Space Port Administration buildings to get rid of him from the planet."

Egdar looked with alarm at Sister Annie. "Why didn't you tell me you were doing this?" he said, "And what is that you are wearing?"

Sister Annie was wearing a silver breastplate and was holding a long pointed metal staff, looking like a strange bag lady.

"I'm channelling Saint Joan of Arc" Sister Annie said.

"Wherefore gird up your loins, be sober and hope to the end for the grace that is to be brought to you," it intoned loudly over the loud speaker.

As Sister Annie was on the loudspeaker and as these words were spoken there was a swell of "Sister Annie, Sister Annie" from the growing crowd.

At the Space Port Planet Manager Redick was stood with three men who had disembarked from the Freighter, and who were surrounded by security men and the Toraxx 9 police when Annie and her followers arrived.

Sister Annie spoke to Redick, "Planet Manager Redick I accuse you of grave and serious crimes against Toraxx 9 and its people. I accuse you of fraud, theft of company profits, dishonesty, deviousness and profiting by slavery. I have proof of all of this, and so do these people with me."

Sister Annie spoke directly to the police standing there. "Arrest this man," she said.

Soon-to-be Ex Planet Manager Redick said "You can't believe this deranged android that was seriously injured not long ago. Arrest it and stop this farce."

The four policemen moved away from Redick as if they were not going to take sides.

One of the men stood next to Redick turned to him and said, "Now it is time for us to take over, I think."

He took a small box out of his pocket and pressed a button. There was a clanking and thumping as something heavy walked out of the freighter unloading bay. It was an enormous armoured robot and it stumped down the ramp towards Sister Annie. The man with the control pressed a button. The robot's arm came up and it fired a missile straight at the android. The small explosive shell hit Sister Annie in the chest armour, was further slowed down by layers of high-tensile fabric and bags of medications, and then stopped by the Toraxx 9-metal cross down the back of its habit.

Before Sister Annie fell it raised its arm with the long rod and fired a burst of high energy at the robot and then quickly at the four men standing in front of it. The robot's electrics fizzled and died, the three tasered men fell and were jumped on by a crush of Sister Annie's followers. Many stood round Sister Annie in shock looking at the large hole in the android's chest.

"Let me through, Let me through," said Egdar.

Later he turned round and said "I cannot save her. Sister Annie is dead."

Swamp workers and hospital patients alike fell to their knees, crying.

The Chaplin spoke, "Brothers and sisters, we must make sure that Sister Annie's sacrifice is not in vain."

Chapter Seven

Egdar Bester and his new android joined the long queue to see the Beatified Sister Annie, heroine of Toraxx 9. Crowds of people shuffled round the large reinforced glass case housing the android, in awe of the sight of the incorruptible body of Sister Annie with the large cavity in its chest. They pushed scraps of paper with their prayers into the mesh protecting the holy android and took small phials of Sister Annie's elixir given free to visitors, ensuring more miracles.

"Even though I love my new body," said Hector, "I really regret not being able to be a nun again. Though I believe that Sister Annie will become a Saint before too long, given the pressure from the Torexx 9 Planet Community Committee. Given the huge shared profits they make they are a heavy pressure group."

"Thanks to you," said Egdar, "And me, of course, because I made you."

"Which reminds me," said Hector, staring up at the wall behind the glass case at the beautiful frescos of winged angels dressed in their wonderful long white smocks, "How would you be with making wings?"

The Secret Inside the Dome City on Envo 4

Chapter One

The survey drone was recording data at the sparse end-quadrant of the spiral arm, the furthest edge of Hundred Planetary Union territory, when it intercepted a distress call from a planet in the Envo system.

Nestor, Chief Executive (and currently the only member) of the Exoanthropology section of the Hundred Planetary Union, was summoned to the office of the President as a 'matter of urgency'.

<< Nestor. There's been a message from the Ecofaith Brethren on Enzo 4 about a massacre about to happen. Return immediately.>>

The President never travelled from the hub – that massive circular space station. Nestor, who preferred to be as unavailable as possible was particularly peeved to have to traverse all 140 segments of moving walkway up to the President's office, and even more peeved when he found he was expected to take a Special Planetary Envoy- fossil brain Lutter – to Envo 4.

Nestor, was senior security adviser for all issues related, however tangentially, to the murky depths of sentient non-human and human hybrids for the Hundred Planetary Union. He was particularly annoyed to have been ordered to "help" the PU envoy to sort out the troubles on Envo 46 as he had acted as Arbiter when the original agreement between the Miners and Builders to work together on Envo 46 was signed seven years ago. At the time he advised the Miners not to proceed and now Nestor had the bleak satisfaction of being proved right. But the thing he was most aggrieved about was that he had been told to deliver a presentation on the background to the conflict for the HoloMedia as news about a rumoured war on Envo 4 has spread quickly. Luckily he had the suitably edited holo he prepared after his last visit to Envo 4 that could be tweaked.

****

Nelly K, Star Mediarist of Interplanetary News turned to

face the lenses. She was attired in her 'serious docunews' outfit of muted cerise and silver spraysuit with only a faint smudge of blue face tint.

"This is Nelly K, reporting for Interplanetary News. So here we are in the outer ring of the Hundred Planetary Union satellite headquarters, and I'm walking up towards the briefing room where Nestor, the famous Exoanthropologist is about to face the media. He is to brief us on the growing threat of imminent war on Envo 46, one of the furthest planets at the edge of known space in the 100PU."

We are now switched to Nelly's EyeLens and we see the huge cladded vaulted tube curving up and away in the distance, with the four-deep varispeed walkways full of people, mechanicals and freight movers.

"Here we are stepping off the walkway into the briefing room. In front of us we can see a raised dais in front of a large vidd space. Nestor has walked in, though he is difficult to see with his long robe, a black bonnet and visor. He is starting the presentation now."

We see Nestor turn briefly to the vidd space and wave his hand.

A voice-over starts as a holo shows the movement of light through space whizzing past planets …

<<As its name tells us, Envo 46 is the fourth of six planets of the star Envo. It is an unexceptional star in the end quadrant of a spiral arm on the Andromeda galaxy.>>

The holo briefly draws back in perspective to show how insignificant Enzo is in the scheme of things. The voice over continues as the holo zooms past Enzo 1 to 3 and focuses on Enzo 4.

<< Envo 46 is overtly unattractive as its oblique tilt and irregular orbit means only an area from the equator to a few degrees north is habitable for a planetary cycle. Formerly covered by rivers the surface now is dusty and dry and Envo's weak oblique rays mean the light is inadequate for growing most crops.

Yet, it has great riches. Initial HPU surveys showed that the planet surface had deep alluvial deposits including diamond bearing conglomerate, and further north other mineral bearing rocks with a wonderful range of silicate gemstones of unusual colours. The HPU Consortium decided to put Envo 4 out to tender for gemstone mining but only for groups who would build settlements and develop the planet for agriculture. Winning the bid were the current leaseholders the EcoFaithBrethren from Envo 3, a colony of scientists, artists and craftworkers wanting to develop the planet's potential, not only through gemstone mining, but also using skills in metallurgy, art and the development of new growing techniques.>>

The holo shows drone footage skimming the brown barren surface of Envo 4 with wind whirling dust into clouds in the low light of an Envo 4 winter. Then it sweeps across the ground to show an excavated cliff with layers of differently coloured earths. A quick shift to a laboratory showing scientists demonstrating a range of mineral ores, and then pictures of a couple of amazing gemstones rippling with rainbow colours when illuminated.

<<So the Miners, unmodified humans from the 3rd planet, acquired the mining lease and future settlement rights if fulfilling their lease agreements. They planned to create and market gemstone crafts and products unique to Envo 4 whilst researching the development of high energy plants able to grow in Envo 4's limiting circumstances. With the agreement of the HPU they also hope to import flora and fauna grown using clean-gene technology. >>

The holo now zooms in and focuses on a group of short, stocky people dressed in thick grey wadded suits inside a large workshop containing an oven or furnace. There is a primitive moving belt carrying what looks like large blocks of mineral ore being gently crushed by a mechanical press, and people are sorting the resulting smaller lumps by hand into containers. A small shovel robot is scooping ore out of a container in to the mouth of the furnace. At the side are piles of small shiny metal ingots.

<<The Miners planned to irrigate the land and realised they needed specialist help to build aquifers from the snow-topped mountains to transport water down to their settlement. They chose the Trem – originally built and leased by the BiomanCorporation. The Trem, in total numbering 30, are mechanically enhanced sapient bioandroids, gene-spliced animal-human hybrids, and technically brilliant builders.>>

The holo now shows a group of people dressed in what look like armoured protective suits standing in front of the dome they are in the process of constructing. These must be the Trem. One of them turns round, it has the too-perfect face of a human, and which we have been told is a human-android construct. Though in these times following HPU Edict 8453 we do not imply in any way that such ortho-humans are inferior to birthed humans.

<<Exoanthropologist Nestor was Arbiter at the contract signed between the Miners and the Builders 7 years ago. The agreement was that the Builders would be entitled to a share of all profits for a period of 5 years, and at the end of the time would leave. At the end of the five year period two years ago the Trem had applied to the HPU for permission to settle on Envo 4 citing their major role in developing the planet and quoting HPU regulations that Envo 4 was well over the area for single species occupation. The miners strongly oppose a Trem settlement. The Trem are refusing to leave. This is the cause of the current dispute.>>

The vidd space goes dark. A spotlight shines on Nestor standing at the lectern. A voice says 'Any Questions for Exoanthropologist Nestor?

Nelly K speaks first. As she speaks a spotlight finds her, showing her outfit to its best advantage.

"CEO Nestor, information obtained by Interplanetary News suggests that the situation in Envo 46 has progressed well beyond a dispute. We believe that the Miners feel threatened and are preparing to fight. How is the HPU going to stop this?"

Nestor replies, his voice sounding bored and annoyed at the same time.

"I have just come from discussions with the President and I can inform you he is sending a Hundred Planetary Union Official Envoy Elf Lutter to Envo 4 to act as Mediator and broker an agreement between the two sides. As I acted as Arbiter to the original agreement I am required to go with and brief the Envoy on the issues affecting the dispute."

Nelly K speaks again.

"CEO Nester, can I suggest that a representative of Interplanetary News attends as part of your delegation to provide a balanced view of this sensitive ongoing situation?"

Luckily we cannot see Nestor's face as his black bonnet shields his face but the fact his voice goes up an octave suggests a certain level of annoyance.

"I will pass your suggestion on to Envoy Lutter who may well appreciate the scrutiny."

Chapter Two

Several days later Zizzy and Bo realised that everyone had gone and left them behind. Em had put them to sleep in their bed-box and in the morning she was gone. The children weren't worried for a day or so, they had left all the children's toys as well as spare boxes of food blocks and jars of water, so they would have to come back for them. In the past Em had often disappeared for days working in the fields or picking up things that had been dumped outside the city walls,

"Perhaps they've gone to get new toys?" said Zizzy hopefully.

The children stood at the cabin door and looked down the muddy rutted track towards the city. As usual the huge dome was cloudy with continually condensing water vapour, and the lower part of the dome obscured by the huge city wall. Up the track, past the other empty cabins, there were no more trucks and caravans.

Bo had a sudden thought. "Where is Henry?"

Zizzy ran round the cabin as fast as her stubby little legs would carry her. "I've found him" she shouted.

On top of the meagre pile of left behind possessions dumped on the twisted roots and stubby leaves of scrubland plants containing heavy metal plant debris, Henry lay face-down. They could tell it was him, because Henry's back was pitted with brown rust and had a big dinge on his leg where Bo had hit him with a metal bar when they were playing. The children were too small to lift him, but Bo found a sheet and tied it round Henry's legs so together they could pull him bit by bit. They managed to drag him the short way to the little hut at the back of the cabin. During the journey a leg dropped off at the knee joint and they found three fingers missing. The hinge on his lower jaw hung loose, giving Henry a hideous grimace.

"Don't look like that, Henry," said Zizzy, and found a doll's blanket to cover his face – and then she realised – "Henry's not working."

"We need to mend him just like Henry tried to mend the cultivator when it broke." said Bo.

Zizzy and Bo went again to stand outside the cabin at the side of the rough track. They looked up at the cluster of rough wood cabins, and past them to the bleak black plain empty now the crop had been harvested, and the path past it to Em's village a long way away. Then they looked down to the blister of the city dome. Zizzy and Bo knew where Henry had gone when he needed to repair something, but the children had never been down the road on their own. They stood for a while undecided. Zizzy did what she always did when she hadn't been told what to do. She practised putting her hands into her little pinny pockets, in-out, in-out. Bo stood frozen. Suddenly he jumped down onto the road and Zizzy followed. She ran after him as fast as she could.

Alfie at Robot Parts and Spares spotted Zizzy and Bo poking around his compound. Wheeling his way over to them he lowered his grabber arms and leaned forward so his communication sensors were close. Zizzy nearly laughed at Alfie's funny jerky voice, but Bo put his hand on her arm to warn her to stay quiet, and said that they wanted to mend Henry who needed a new leg.

"Which model HNR1 is it?" asked Alfie. "I want to buy late model HNR1s."

"I don't know" said Bo, suddenly worried, "he's very very old".

"Look inside the breastplate," advised Alfie, "The number will be written underneath. I may want to buy old models for spares." Alfie ticked for a few minutes before having a bright idea. "You bring me old robots and I'll let you have parts for Henry."

Back at the cabin they struggled to prop Henry up. Bo

rooted in the pile of debris and found a knife. Twiddling it round and round like he had seen Da do, he opened the hatch on Henry's chest, and saw 'HNR1 679', and a red button. Pressed it. Henry's eyes opened.

Words tumbled out, "Henry you've lost a leg and some fingers. We need to mend you. Alfie says if we take him robots we can get a new leg for you." Bo waited but Henry didn't move.

Zizzy got fed up of waiting for something to happen and went to look for things in the pile of junk. Bo sat by Henry until it almost started to go dark. A ping signalled Henry's reboot: he sat up and snapped his jaw back into position. Zizzy gleefully arrived back waving two of the missing fingers and went back to look for the third. Later the children sat quietly by Henry as he told them what they needed to do next, though his voice was a bit funny and wobbly.

Early the morning after, Henry slowly cobbled together a little two-wheeled trolley using Zizzy's old doll's pram. He managed to do the work leaning on the discarded crowbar that Bo found rusting at the bottom of the pile of stuff in the garden. Henry then lifted the cultivator robot onto the trolley and the children set off down the road to Alfie's Parts and Spares dragging the trolley in little jerks.

Alfie's was a little distance outside the city walls which was pretty lucky as Henry had warned them about children being kidnapped in the city. Alfie rolled over to them and examined the cultivator robot with his delicate pincer fingers on his grabber arm.

"Not much call for these now, but it has the same impeller device as some cleaning robots, so I can use it for spares." It said. Bo asked for the supplies Henry wanted.

Later as they were going Alfie said, "What model is your HNR1?"

"592," said Bo, giving the number Henry had told him to.

"It is no use to me," said Alfie. "Too old".

Alfie studied them carefully putting its communication

sensors up close. "How old are you children?"

Fed up of being ignored Zizzy answered something she DID know. "I'm three and nearly four and Bo is seven."

"People pay for little children," said Alfie, Bo started to pull Zizzy away, "so keep hidden near the city."

They had managed to get the supplies Henry wanted so now the children set off tugging the trolley back up the hill. Henry had dragged himself into the cabin when they got back with the leg and other spares he needed. But he was not able to mend himself. His voice was very slurred and they were very worried about him.

"Don't.....worry.....energy   ....level.....low. Need....to....switch.....off. Go....to..bed...and....hide."

Night came early on Envo 4 in winter. Zizzy and Bo, with Henry switched off and propped up against the wall, got into their bed-box on the shelf to hide.

Light came slowly into the cabin. It had been quiet during the night, but now there was a gust of wind shushing dust and small pebbles onto the window. There was no warning shadow across the window, but a bright light suddenly shone into the room, stopped for moment on Henry, and then disappeared.

Bo helped Zizzy down from the bed-box, and they sorted through their outfits to choose coats and shoes for travelling. Then they both packed their clothes and a favourite toy into a small case. Bo had remembered Da telling them that they needed to be somewhere safe for winter, and if Henry couldn't help, and they were in trouble, they should go to the Dome city.

Holding hands, they walked slowly down to the Dome City. It was surrounded by city walls with a metal gate in the wall. There was a red light in what looked like a button, high up on the gate. Bo knew they would have to press it, but they were too small. They put down their luggage.

Outside the walls were piles of discarded rubbish left behind by the miners at the end of summer and sorted through by scavengers. Zizzy and Bo found boxes and piles of stones and made a pile of stuff. When it was high enough Bo climbed on top and Zizzy scrambled up his back and stood on his shoulders like they had played lots of times. Finally, she was high enough to press the red button.

BONG. It wasn't so much a loud noise, more a noise and a vibration. They waited.

"Press it again," said Bo. BONG.

Silently, the gate opened. A tall person dressed in a silver suit looked at the edifice in front of him.

"Who have we here?" he asked.

"Zizzy and Bo" said Bo, "And we have come for you to help us, because Da said we should."

The silver man lifted Zizzy, then Bo, down from their perch, and carefully cleared away the pile of stuff they were standing on. Then he lifted Zizzy onto his shoulders, and Bo under one arm, and picked up both their cases in the other hand, to take them into the city.

"Stop," said Zizzy. "We need to save Henry who needs mending and he's switched himself off."

"We will look after you first, and then go and save Henry," said the silver man, "By the way, my name is Trev."

112

Chapter Three

Held firmly in the carrying web, Nestor whiled away the journey time counting the flick of photons escaping from who knows where on the cladding of the ship's AI.

<<You're leaking. Twenty-seven particles in the last two seconds. How long before we reach Envo 4 orbit? >>

<<I assume you want that in standard time rather than particles to count? If so, we will be in range within six ship hours. I am preparing to send in the drone as per your instructions as soon as we reach orbit.>>

Nestor pondered.

<<Better wake up His Excellence. Give him an hour and then turn up the heat>>

The ship's AI emitted something not unlike a dry cough.

<<Bit severe>>

<<But I want him unsettled, less likely to try to take decisions. The skill will be to make him think he's in charge>>

The ship's AI spoke again,

<<What about Interplanetary News Reporter Nelly K? She requested to be wakened on arrival.>>

<<Wake her early as well. An hour after the Envoy.>>

Nestor rummaged in his flight bag and came out with a ball of fur and a comb, and then spent a pleasant time planning his strategy and grooming, whilst a small pink tongue licked his fingers.

Much later the Envoy shuffled into the forward cabin wrapped in a thermal heating wrap and sucking a booster pastille. Nestor could smell his faint purple aura triggering a sharp taste of citrus - a sure sign of incipient liver overload.

"Your Excellence, fit yourself into the net and I will brief you about the dispute whilst the medibot adjusts your body fluids." Nestor said in his most ingratiating tone (which wasn't very).

"Can't this wait? The ship told me that we have almost two days before planetfall," the Envoy squeaked.

"Ah! But we are expecting a vidd message from the Chair of the Miner's Council once we get in range and I thought you would want to be prepared."

"Of course." The Envoy tried to gain his composure.

<<Vidd message? News to me Nestor>>

<<There will be one – get onto Enzo 4's Council and set it up>>

Nestor began his plan to brief Envoy Lutter.

"Well, your Excellency, I did explain before we set off that this is the worst time to be visiting this primitive rock planet. It is almost at aphelion of its irregular orbit, and into its long winter. It will be very cold. The extreme oblique angle of Envo's rays mean that the only plant life-the primitive algae and tree-like bryophytes (there is a particularly massive liverwort I believe in the northern hemisphere) are struggling to turn out oxygen in the diminished light, sometimes requiring the humans to wear rebreathers."

The Envoy's eyes were already glazing over and Nestor moved into part B

"I realise that it is all a great deal to absorb all at once, so I have brought a recorded holo of my presentation with a vocnote for your wrist comms screen so you can refer to key points when you need to."

Special Envoy Elf Lutter was asleep and swaying gently in his net before five minutes of the holo had played.

Later Interplanetary News Reporter Nelly K shuffled into the cabin: she was a wreck, dressed in another lurid skinsuit with her hair stood on end and shaking with cold.

Nestor looked at her with amused concern.

115

"Is this your first time in a freezeflight?"

Nelly K nodded. Nestor asked the AI to get a spare warm suit from a crew member. Nelly K zipped herself into the oversize drab grey suit when it arrived, but with only her face showing she couldn't decide whether she was pleased to be warm, or annoyed to be so totally cancelled.

"Nelly K fit yourself into the net and the medibot will adjust your body fluids." Nestor said in his not very ingratiating and patronising tone, "We are waiting for a Vidd message from the Council of Miners at Envo 4 to update us on the current situation."

<<Envo 4 asking to open vidd channel>>

<<Prepare them to connect. Blow cold air on our visitors to get them ready for the transmission>>

<<Bit severe>>

<<So what are you – the temperature control police?>>

Nestor raised his voice.

"Envoy Lutter, Nelly K, the transmission from Envo 4 is nearly ready to go live.!"

Two heads with bleary eyes swivelled towards Nestor, he gestured towards the screen which had started flickering.

Nestor mind-linked with the ship's AI.

<<Keep me out of sound and vision in this exchange>>

<<You are up to something Nestor!>>

The screen cleared and now showed a group of people wearing grey warmsuits. There were two stood at the front and clearly going to act as spokespeople, and one of them appeared to be in the late stages of pregnancy. Most of the group seemed to be carrying poles, or possibly (surely unlikely?) spears. The Miner's representative spoke.

"Is that the Hundred Planetary Union Envoy Lutter? We have been informed he is on his way. Are you there?"

"Yes," answered Lutter,"I am Special Envoy Lutter, and I

have Nelly K here with me, reporting for the HoloMedia. You can tell us your current situation."

"I am Jonas," said the representative, "Head of the EcoFaithBrethren, and this is Emily, my wife. We are armed and are preparing to confront the Trem to clear them off our planet."

"Are there any particular issues that make you feel you have to be violent?" asked the Envoy.

"They have been taking our children," shouted Emily.

"As you can see," said Jonas pushing his wife forward, "Several of our wives are expecting babies, and we are concerned that the Trem will want to take our babies. We want you to make them hold to their agreement and leave."

The vidd transmission was terminated by Envo 4.

Nelly K, was suddenly animated, "I need a Holo Channel through to Interplanetary News, our viewers will be shocked to hear the news of Androids stealing human babies."

"I am sorry but we are currently unable to transmit to the HPU or IN headquarters. But don't you think it is strange that this is the first time we have heard this accusation? In a case of a two-way dispute, don't we need to hear both sides?" said Nestor.

"Nestor is correct," said Envoy Lutter. Slow-thinker he might be, but he knew the rules in a dispute, "We need to hear what the Trem have to say about this accusation."

<<What's this about being unable to transmit>>

<<We will be when you switch the channel off for a little while. This accusation could launch an Interplanetary conflict.>>

"We need to call on the Trem," said Envoy Lutter, "without announcing our visit, to stop them trying to hide anything."

"I will take my camera," said Nelly K.

"Yes, recording only," said Envoy Lutter, "but no transmission without HPU agreement."

<<So, landing at Trem City. Lucky the Domes are easy to spot, even from here. Tell our guests we will be landing in around 26 hours. Time for more sleep, no doubt.>>

Chapter Four

Trev took Zizzy and Bo into the Dome, the paths were nice and flat, and Zizzy could skip ahead to look at the smaller Domes as they passed. Eventually, Trev stopped and touched the side of one of the smaller domes, and a door opened.

"Come on in and meet my wife Teri," then he said, "Teri, here are another two abandoned children." Inside there was another tall silver person. Who when she saw Zizzy and Bo rushed over to meet them.

"Oh, you poor, dear children," she said, "You must have been so lonely."

"Well, usually Henry looks after us," said Zizzy, "But now he's broken."

"I promised to go and look at Henry," Trev told his wife, "And we can collect more of your clothes and toys, because we can't make those things," he said to Zizzy and Bo.

When Trev saw Henry he realised he was mendable, but would need his energy cells charging.

Zizzy and Bo collected more of their toys and clothes and collapsible bed-box and Trev put them all in a pack on his back.

He then bent down to speak to the children.

"Henry needs mending. If I take him, you have got to help.

"

The children said they really, really, wanted to help, so Trev lifted Henry up, and held his body under one arm, with his spare leg under the other.

"Come on, Brother Henry," he said.

When they returned to the Dome, Trev put Henry on the floor, and put Zizzy and Bo's bed-box on a shelf.

"Where is Teri?" asked Zizzy.

"She's having a bath," said Trev. He showed Zizzy and Bo the 'bath' at the edge of the dome. Beautifully fashioned from marble, but full of what looked like green scum. No sign of Teri, but there was an empty silver suit on the floor next to the bath.

"Where is Teri?" Bo asked.

"In the bath under the water," answered Trev. He went on to explain how the Trem, partly made with living tissue, could dry out in a place like Envo 4, so they needed to refresh in plant cells every few days to keep fit.

"Can we have a bath?" asked Bo.

"Sorry," said Trev, "You are not made like us."

Then Trev began to repair Henry, and Zizzy was given the task of removing the rust from its body. She leant over the robot and rubbed and rubbed until the brown rust was gone. Bo had to oil the creaking joints whist Trev fixed the legs and charged up the energy storage. Trev let Bo open the breastplate and press the button for starting. Eventually Henry's eyes opened and it stood up smoothly without creaking.

"Henry, say thank you to Trev for mending you," said Zizzy, "And for saving us as well, "added Bo.

"Henry, why don't you take Zizzy and Bo into the big Dome to look around," said Trev, "I need a bath."

Zizzy and Bo told Henry of all their adventures after he had stopped working. The three of them saw other silver people looking out of their small domes as they walked around. None of them looked surprised to see them, but then they didn't know that the Trem could mind-talk to each other.

In the centre of the big Dome was an open area, with what looked like a children's playground. That was because it was a children's playground and as they reached it a number of children, all about their own age, ran out to play. There were swings, a roundabout, two climbing frames and a sand pit with a digging machine. Within two minutes Henry couldn't even see where Zizzy and Bo were any more, they had disappeared into the throng of children. The robot sat down on a bench to wait, after all, his job was to watch over them. One or two Trem came to sit down next to him.

Chapter Five

HPU Envoy Lutter's party, swaddled in their unfamiliar warmsuits, got into the planet lander, in the hold of Nestor's Space Ship. Nestor, with light body-armour, covered by his black cloak followed them into the Lander at the last minute squeezing into the travel-net at the back.

After the little flyer manoeuvred out of the hold, Nestor mind-linked with his AI comms in the Ship.

<<Keep scanning for any sign of the Miners approaching the Trem Dome, and let me know if you sight them. I don't expect either group will start a physical confrontation but if there is any sight of it, use the light stun to deter them. You can set us down as near to the door of the Dome as you can>>

<<I hope you know what you are doing here. You are putting the Envoy and the Mediarist in the middle of an unpredictable, possibly dangerous, situation. You are going to be found out, Nestor>>

<<Go on, cheer me up. You're always such a killjoy. And very pushy for a collection of electronic pulses. By the way, I do know what is going to happen, and it will mean Special Envoy Lutter and Nelly K of Interplanetary News will have all the fame they want>>

<<I hope that is fame in a good way>>

<<Oh you of little faith>>

Nestor tuned into a conversation Envoy Lutter was having with Nelly K.

"And if we go into the Trem Dome I want you to keep behind me, so I can protect you."

Nelly K was incensed, "Envoy Lutter, I need to be first in because I am vidding for the world to see."

"But only when I give you permission, as I said, you need to be behind me."

Nestor broke in.

"With respect, HPU Special Envoy, I need to meet the Trem first, as I already know them, and I can guarantee your safety."

<<You hope>>

As they started final descent, with the roar of the landing jets, drowning conversation, Nestor got another message from his AI.

<<A small ground-flitter has just left the Miner's village, and a group of Miners have also set off walking from the village down to the Dome city. We will get there before them>>

The HPU Special Envoy's party arrived at the Trem Dome. To be truthful, Envoy Lutter was really quite scared, going into what might be a fraught confrontation without armed support officers. He would never have agreed to this if he had known. As a result he was happy for Nestor to go first, and stayed several paces behind. Nelly K bent to the side of him so her EyeLens could vidd what was happening.

"Can I start to vidd now?" asked Nelly K. "No," said Envoy Lutter, "I said not until I tell you."

The Dome door opened as Nestor arrived. A tall silver suited figure stood there.

"Hello Trev," said Nestor

"Nice to see you again, Arbiter Nestor," said Trev." Who is that with you?"

"Can I introduce Special Envoy Lutter, and Mediarist for Interplanetary News Nelly K. They are here to find out about your dispute with the Miners."

And then, in mind-link, he said to Trev.

<<The Miners are on their way, so I suggest you let us in and close the door for a while>>

Trev led the Envoy's party into the Dome and took them through to the central open space where other Trem were standing, as well as an old, but shiny, robot.

"Let me introduce you to my wife, Teri, my Deputy Crev, and his wife Ceri." Hands were shaken.

Envoy Lutter was stunned, in a whisper, he said to Nelly K out of the corner of his mouth, "They are all identical androids. How can they have wives?"

Trev heard Envoy Lutter's question, and answered, "We Trem can choose our gender depending on which best fits our personality."

Nelly K asked Trev, "Is that a children's playground? "

"Yes," said Teri, "Do you want to see the children?"

"You can start vidding now," Envoy Lutter said to Melly K.

Around a dozen little children came out of the various small Domes, and rushed onto the playground.

"So it's true, " said Envoy Lutter.

Just then the gate bell sounded. BONG.

"Wait here, I'll go and just let Jonas and Emily in," said Nestor.

When Jonas, Emily and Nestor arrived back, the Miners seemed particularly subdued.

"See," said Emily quietly, "I told you they had our children."

Nestor called out, "Henry, please bring Zizzy and Bo here to us."

The robot went up to the children and turned round holding the hands of a little girl and a little boy.

As soon as the children saw Nestor they started shouting "Da! Da!" and the little girl Zizzy ran up to Nestor who scooped her up into his arms, and patted the boy, Bo's head.

"No," said Nestor, "These are not YOUR children Emily - they are MY children. They are specialist child androids made to my specification and brought here for you. In those early years when you arrived you told me that conditions in the colony were not fit yet to raise children, but during the winters you longed to have children to look after, to stop you feeling too homesick. But as you started to have your own children, things changed, didn't they?"

"Da! Da!" interrupted Zizzy patting Nestor's cheeks with her little hands, "Stop talking and let me go. We want to play!"

"Wait a minute, my dear little person," said Nestor. "I want you and Bo to tell us why you came here to the Dome, when I left you with Emily and Henry to look after you."

"Em left us in the bed-box," said Zizzy, "and then went away."

"We found Henry broken on a heap of rubbish behind the cabin." said Bo.

"And his leg fell off when we tried to move him, so he was broken." Interrupted Zizzy as usual.

"It was winter, and we didn't know what to do. So we came here and we are staying with Trev and Teri. Trev mended Henry and we love playing with the children." finished Bo.

"Can we stay here Da?" asked Zizzy.

Nestor turned to Envoy Lutter who was looking quite bewildered.

"I think, your Excellency, that the accusation of children being stolen is clearly not true."

"Em," said Nestor, "Why did you abandon the children when you left the cabin?"

Emily answered "As you know the android children are inactivated, probably charging or something when you put them in the box. Because of this we just put them away for the winter. They are not human, and they were perfectly safe. The Trem stole all these children here that you gave to us."

Trev stepped forward and spoke loudly and with feeling, "We did not steal any of the children. These wonderful little persons were specially made to be companions to humans. Like us, they do not need to sleep and can be active day and night. However, humans sleep during the night so these children were programmed to sleep for 12 hours every night when they were put in the bed-box, and again if they are put in the box, two hours in the afternoon like human children. At the end of the summer Miners who were expecting their own babies, or those already with babies chose to put away their android "toys". The day after they left the children would get out of the box and look around, not sure what to do. If we found abandoned children (usually an older boy and younger girl) wandering about we brought them here. What the Miners failed to appreciate was that these are not just animated dolls. These are very sophisticated little people who will always remain the same age. but who are constantly capable of learning new things and remain funny and innocent. The children fill a huge gulf in our lives, and they are happy with us." Trev sat down obviously upset.

Nelly K had managed to get a close up of this impassioned speech, and had not noticed a little boy walking up to her. He took a handful of her warmsuit and tugged it.

Nelly K looked down, her EyeLens vidding a close up of the boy. "Hello," she said "What's your name?"

"I'm Dan," he said, "Can I have a look through your camera, please?"

Nelly K was charmed and let him look through the Lens for a few seconds. "I'm taking vidds for a lot of people to see. Do you want to speak some words to them?"

"Hello," said Dan. "If you visit me I will let you play with my toys." Nelly K realised this was such good viddvision she carried on talking to the little ones.

Nestor quietly said to Trev and Jonas. "I don't think the children are the source of your conflict, are they?"

Jonas looked away, and it was Teri who answered.

"Our agreement with the Miners, that you witnessed, was

that we should have half profits for five years. We know the Miners have refined many hundreds of tons of ore, and yet they tell us they have not made a profit for five years. We know they are stockpiling not only the rough gemstones, but also their finished crafts. We built a large warehouse for them three years ago, and we know it is now full. We told them, if the Miners pay us our half of the profits, we will leave this planet and find another one wanting to welcome a small number of superb builders, and their young friends.'"

Envoy Lutter, accompanied by Nelly K and her camera, went in the flyer to see the warehouse, and discovered the Trem had told the truth. The Miners tried to argue that the Trem were heathens, and not even human, and anyway, they didn't need the money. Envoy Lutter found their pleas to be insulting, and the Miners were ordered to pay the Trem their due, and at the same time said he would consult the Hundred Planetary Union whether it was appropriate to cancel their lease.

All this was captured by Nelly K and now approved for transmission by Envoy Lutter – though it would need editing given the sheer amount of footage of the children playing and hugging her warmsuit. She was going to have a quiet word with Nestor later.

Back on the ship and on the way home, Nestor's AI commed him.

<<You were lucky you didn't get found out>>

<<You must be joking. The President thinks it is in his best interest to keep it quiet. After all, I am a much older model than the Trem. I was a prototype and am still unique>>

<<You know what they say 'Pride comes before a fall'. You might not get away with keeping things to yourself another time. Shipping in young children used to be called slavery>>

<<Bit severe>>

Cry Havoc and Let TimeSlide the Bots of War

Chapter One

It's dark when she wakes up with a throbbing headache. Her eyes take a while to get used to seeing in the low light. She's cold, and feels to be lying on something hard. A feeble light comes on and looking up and to the side when she manages to focus, she can see it's a small narrow room. She moves slightly. There is a crackling sound, and lifting up her arms she can see the noise is made by strips of her epidermis sloughing off, a sudden thought- like a snake shedding its skin.

"Where am I?" she says, not too loud, it may be dangerous, and then, suddenly she thinks …

"Who am I?" There is no answer.

Slowly she sits up, the thin cover over her falls off. No wonder she is cold, she is wearing only her underwear and a blue theatre gown. When she tries to sit up her head feels so dizzy she falls back again, but out of the corner of her eye she notices that there is a table with some things piled on top of it.

Later, swivelling her legs onto the floor, she stands up slowly and takes a step towards the table. There is a folded coverall, several bottles of water and pouches of, she supposes, food. A sip of water causes a severe coughing fit. Sitting back on what she recognises as a trolley, she starts to brush off the strips of her dried skin covered in some sort of pink coating, but stops as she sees the flesh underneath is red and swollen. Like sunburn, she thinks. If she sits still she finds her head doesn't hurt as much, but running her hands through her hair she discovers that there is a metal net underneath. It is firmly attached to her skull.

"Who put this effing thing on my head? "she shouted.

There was no answer, and the shout echoed around the room. Realising that whoever put the net on her head may be still around waiting for her to wake up, she had a rising feeling of panic, and thought…'I've got to get out of here.'

As she is struggling to put on the overlarge coverall, she

hears a sigh 'Shhh', the sound of the door opening. Her heart is nearly jumping out of her chest. What if someone is waiting outside? Thinking that whatever happened she didn't want to stay imprisoned in this room any longer, she tottered to the door, and pulled it open. There was no one there, at least as far as she could see with the ground sloping away. As the stress subsides a little, a sensation of roughness on her feet makes her realise: she is wearing no shoes. If she wants to go somewhere she needs shoes, food and water. Walking slowly back into the room she eventually finds a pair of trainers that fit her (Are these mine?) and a backpack under the table. Packing a couple of bottles of water and several pouches she takes another drink of water, no choking this time.

Holding onto the door jamb with one hand, she steps outside and can see she is on hillside. Tottering down the slope a little way, she looks back. Behind her set into the slope, are four doors – the door she came through is open and the others are closed. Someone else could be coming out soon. The feeling of panic rises again. It is too steep to try to walk further up the hillside, so she walks unsteadily downhill for a little way. She can see the hillside levelling out at the bottom onto a flat plain, burnt grass leading along to the seashore. She could be anywhere.

Then she hears a faint loudspeaker announcement, "Come immediately to your Embarkation Point."

Staring at the sandy shore, she notices that there is something sticking up into the sky. There are some ladders. Ladders leading up into the sky until they disappear from sight. Has everyone gone and left her behind?

She turns and walks unsteadily back, but then trips and falls forward up the slope.

Mavis was totally disoriented when she woke up. Her last memory was of standing at the window in her room in the island pub playing cards with a Carebot (nobody could call her prejudiced about robots, though she was fed up of always losing - if the bots really cared they would arrange for her to win sometimes). She couldn't feel if her cards were still in her pocket as there appeared to be something wrapping her hands. Suddenly a light came on and she saw she was in a small corridor, lying on a table, with a cover over her.

'Am I in prison? What did I do wrong?' she asked herself.

Mavis sat up and turned round, and the cover dropped on the floor. Underneath she appeared to be wearing a hospital gown. So she must be in hospital? Then there was a click and a Shhh. The door blew open with the wind and bright sunlight shone in. She saw that her hands and lower arms were covered in what looked and felt like metal gauntlets, but the substance they were made of was quite thin and flexible. Her hands hurt, so Mavis tried to peel the stuff off, but the thin metal material was stuck down. On the table next to her, was a folded tracksuit, a pair of shoes, a backpack and two bottles of water. Given her arthritis and the things on her hands it was a struggle to get down off the trolley and dressed. Afterwards she managed to put the couple of bottles of water into the backpack, and only a bit wobbly she walked to the door and looked out. She could see down a hillside in front of her. How on earth did she get here? As she watched she noticed a figure walking unsteadily up the hill towards her.

Chapter Two

When the men got off the ferry the islanders thought, at first, that they were walkers or birdwatchers, even though this was highly unlikely in January. Later, when observed using measuring equipment, Wilf was not so much curious, but alarmed.

"What are you doing here?" he asked.

One of the men got a card out of his wallet, it had his picture and authorisation.

"M.O.D.," he said. We're doing surveys of a number of islands for the Ministry of Defence. We'll be out of your way in a few hours."

A helicopter came to pick them up.

Nothing else happened for the next two months, and the islanders thought the problem had gone away, but one morning in March a large freight helicopter landed on the island to deliver earth moving equipment and soldiers.

Before the war, the 43 islanders were glad to be living a healthy, bucolic agricultural subsistence lifestyle (albeit with weekly deliveries from the mainland). Surrounded by over 200 miles of ocean, they were well out of the way, so they thought, from rumblings of hostilities between clusters of nations posturing against each other. That was until one army decided to set up a military base on the island.

"You're our MP, can't you stop them building a base here?"

"I'm sorry, where there is an argument for 'defence of the realm' they are allowed to requisition facilities. It's only a small company of army engineers. "

"The upset is going to disturb the birds during the nesting season, and will mean that the tourist season is cancelled."

"I'm advised that the birds will settle down quickly after a small disturbance, and tourists can arrive as usual for a while. You will, of course, be reimbursed for any loss."

The engineers excavated an opening into the mountainside west of the town, creating a tunnel which broke through into the large cave in the limestone cliff. After a further helicopter delivery, military headquarters were built inside the cliff. These included living and storage space for soldiers and ordnance, and extended to small drone hangars and missile tunnels. At some point during the building two amphibious stealth needle subs, holding top-secret cargo, arrived at night into the sea cave in a cove at the south west of the island.

The engineers created an island intranet with two AI Nodes. One a 'Data Soak' with massive online and offline military and other major information resources, to manage all secure communications from and to the island, as well as overseeing all day-to-day military activities within the island. This resource was called MAIN (Management AI Node) and the second network node left for the operation of internal activities related to the islanders. This was twinned to the military network and both driven by a bank of solar panels and two large island wind turbines, supplemented by the hydroelectric wave-power generator they installed.

In September, after these were completed, the senior officer, Major Sperling, approached Mavis, the pub landlady and asked, "Who do I speak to about island matters? Who's in charge?"

"Nobody," she answered, "All the islanders pretty well want to speak for themselves – and then there are the bird wardens and tourists in the hotel next door."

"Can you spread the message for everyone interested to assemble in the Community Hall on Saturday 19.00 your time, when Major Sperling will be available to brief everyone on the work we will be doing and answer any questions we can. Tourists intending to travel to the island have been informed that the ferry returning to the mainland on Saturday morning will be the last to take people from the island for some time. Please can you also inform the tourists in the hotel."

On Saturday evening everybody on the island and their dog were waiting in the community hall, facing the small raised platform complete with covered-up easel. Eventually the noise hushed as the rear door opened, then a loud gasp as three figures entered. The gasp because one of the figures was obviously a robot. Grey metal and around 1.75 m tall, smaller than the two soldiers and with a blank, expressionless, but nonetheless humanoid, face. One soldier stepped forward.

"My name is Major Sperling and I'm the officer in charge of this military research base. On my left is Sergeant Howard, my second in command currently in charge of logistics and stores, and this is an ancillary bot. We don't always name our bots, but this one is called Apollo."

Major Sperling went on to tell the varied group of people currently on the island that the military company, at that time, consisted of technical specialists involved in monitoring communications and soldiers ensuring their safety. He confirmed that, for security reasons, no civilians could leave the island for, at least, the next few months (in exceptional circumstances a military helicopter may be used for transfer). In addition, the military would give islanders access to their high-speed network, but all communications from and to the island would be monitored. In cases where there were shortages of food or essential supplies, such as drugs or medications, then a list should be left for Sergeant Howard at the island shop. Sergeant Howard then removed the cover from the easel. There was a topological map of the island with several areas shaded.

"Our base will be off-limits to all islanders," he said, " these shaded areas show the other restricted places, including the northern rock face and beach, and the south west area of the island next to the base." He then added, "Are there any questions? Give your name before you ask, please."

"Wilf Jackson, crofter. What right do you have to impose these restrictions on us?"

The Major replied, "Information we possess suggests that War could break out on a number of fronts in the next few months. The intelligence work we are undertaking could be critical to the outcome. One of the things we will do here is to help you to be protected against any enemy action."

"Chris Corner, Bird Warden. We need to go on the northern cliffs to monitor the birds. How can you stop us ringing birds in the nesting season?"

"Mr Corner, let us just wait to see what happens before the nesting season."

Several more questions were answered and Lucy got bored. She turned to Mavis, the pub landlady, who was sat next to her and said, "I wonder if Major Posh is married?" The question just happened to hit the air at a quiet time. Everybody heard, and turned to look at her. She turned purple with embarrassment.

As they were walking out of the centre there was a soft touch on Lucy's arm. It was the 'bot', Apollo.

"All the soldiers were required to be single," it said in a pleasant voice. "Even me." Apollo appeared to close one eye. Was this an audacious wink or an electronic glitch?

Some crofts already had stone-lined root cellars under their small cottages, but the soldiers extended the storage cellar underneath the Community Hall 'just in case' it was needed for a bomb shelter.

Meanwhile....

In one of the largest spaces inside the mountain the TechMeldbots have set up their laboratory. They are having problems replicating the conditions they need to switch and adapt their Space Project. This involves research augmenting Satellite GPS Technology by developing 'master clocks' that would provide PNT (Position, Navigation, Timing) in the absence of GPS signals. There have been considerable difficulties stabilising the lab environment so their quantum photonics computing will remain unaffected by electrical and magnetic fields. Effectively they are trying to build up a ytterbium -171 optical clock where 'ticks' of the rapidly oscillating ytterbium laser are counted by complex technology-and all of this to be contained in a small, portable case. There will need to be several antennas, spaced several hundred miles apart, reading and comparing signals from outer space in order to calibrate a laboratory-sized optical clock before they can start to make it smaller.

The only member of the military on the island to have any idea at all of the complexity of what the TechMeldbots are trying to achieve is Sergeant Hanne Stohl, a physics graduate before her army career. Even Hanne is not fully aware of the implications of their research, and as the liaison officer between the TechMeld and Major Sperling, she is in a difficult situation. Her primary role is to supervise the Island Intranet, both the secure military net and civilian link, but most importantly monitor and safeguard the MAIN.

Chapter Three

Islanders could increasingly hear aeroplanes or drones flying high in the clouds above the island, and light flashes were seen in the sky at night. As the possibilities of War escalated, with several countries increasing military build-up, Major Sperling called another meeting with the islanders. This time, as well as Sergeant Howard, he was joined by a further two soldiers, and four bots.

After initial greetings and a warning that threat levels of War were increased to 'high' he began to introduce the personnel based on the island who would be the liaison in the unlikely event there were direct threats to the island.

"You have already met myself and Sergeant Howard, and here is Sergeant Engineer Hanne Stohl who fitted the island intranet, and Private Marcus Blake, who is now your liaison with us, and next to them are three ancillary bots and Julius, a Techbot" The large bot, a dull matt black and a fraction taller than the soldiers, nodded to the islanders.

"These larger bots, we refer to as Techbots, are our technical research officers, with specific vital intelligence roles, and this military base is here with the prime tasks of protecting them and the work they are doing. But, in addition, we have now allocated three of our ancillary bots to islander support. They are trained paramedics and we are re-naming them Carebots, each will have access to electric vehicles. You will possibly already have already met Apollo and the other two are Pan and Ajax."

WW4 came sooner than expected, was devastating, mutually destructive and pretty well all over bar the shouting after two months, though it dragged on in sporadic skirmishes on larger land masses. It was estimated that up to 90% of the World's population had been exterminated with the firestorm leaving the green earth blackened with the crust riven with enormous craters. Countries had not fully realised that developing massive weapons that didn't poison the atmosphere with radioactivity, meant there were no longer deterrents in place to limit their use by unhinged dictators. Or so-called sane leaders tied into retaliation. The weapons developed not only laid waste to infrastructure, habitations, land and landscapes, but also fired tiny fleches that pierced skin and rotted both human and animal flesh. Not to mention specifically targeted devices that destroyed sight and hearing.

Almost forgotten on the edge of hostilities, the island had suffered only a glancing attack on the south east of the island by a Firedrone at the end of its trajectory, and a direct hit above the northern cliff face by a SonicFlash bomb which damaged three buildings in the town, reduced one to rubble, and killed off the nesting bird colony. Islanders who were not in safe spaces, were killed. Island missiles were fired with codes provided by headquarters on the mainland, to targets in the west trialling guidance technology developed by the TechMeld. All the surveillance drones were eventually shot down but not before sending back vital information to headquarters, which helped but only in the short term. The stealth needle crafts went on many sorties to place beacons and buoys; traversing oceans and seas to the west, east and north placing antennas on land enabling calibration of the optical 'master clock' of the TechMeld. One unit returned in a needle craft with seriously injured soldiers and two damaged ancillary bots. A boatload of refugees from the mainland, all suffering from exposure and burns, arrived at the Island.

Major Sperling finally recognised that the War was over and the human race lost, when MAIN confirmed that Headquarters had gone off air and all electronic networks were down with undersea cables severed. TechMeld-enabled technology allowed vids to be downloaded from cameras on Moon Base. These showed an earth, no longer green, but mostly dark brown and black. Close ups of world cities showed no signs of life monitored over weeks.

After the War the priority on the island was to move all the injured, combatants and civilians, into the army hospital, run by

143

the military surgeon and ancillary bots. An extension was built on the island hotel and those needing care and recuperation were moved into it.

Eventually, the stunned island population, and the reluctantly-now-resident remaining military personnel, realised they were all stuck together on the island for the foreseeable time ahead. Winter driving rainstorms and high winds, made living on the island uncomfortable and within six months both groups found their ideas for the future management of the island and its stored resources -mainly the military stockpiles and bot deployments- were seriously incompatible. (Besides which Major Sperling knew he had too few of his people fit and ready to take charge even though the major resources belonged to the army). They finally agreed that Sergeant Howard and Wilf Jackson would work together to act as the island police. They had considerable difficulties in agreeing with each other, never mind keeping the peace.

"What's the problem?" said Wilf and the Sergeant addressing the jostling group outside the pub, as if they couldn't guess.

Two ancillary bots lay decapitated on the floor and five soldiers were trying to protect their two mechanically-repaired colleagues as the islander group moved menacingly towards them.

"We are refusing to have any bots or cyborgs frightening the women in the pub," one man shouted," And the military aren't welcome in town anyway," added another.

"Where do you think the beer and spirits in the pub are coming from?" said a soldier. "That will stop if you ban us coming into the town."

Sergeant Howard knew how contentious his threat to beer supplies would be, and Wilf reluctantly agreed how unacceptably bigoted the islander's viewpoint was. After a few minutes consultation with Wilf a compromise was suggested and accepted. The soldiers would have their own bar provided in the Island Hotel, they would stay away from the pub, and alcohol would continue to be provided for the islanders. The soldiers said that islanders were welcome to join them at their bar as long as there would be no further name-calling of any kind.

"Can't I carry on seeing my army boyfriend?" asked Nola, obviously distraught at the idea of segregation.

"No! Absolutely NOT," her father answered, pulling her away.

As well as such incidents, the military had to remain patient and unruffled during demonstrations from the original island population, who didn't want to accept what they were told about the War and its aftermath. One or two migrants from the mainland demanded to be 'taken back home' and refused to believe vid footage shown to them.

Techbot communications

<<MELD query: Why are humans wiping themselves off the Earth?>>

<<JuliusMELD: Many theories but as humans are tribal there have always been conflicts over desire of one tribe to dominate others or take over resources but once wars start there can be a chain reaction of retaliation>>

Techbot Julius' role in the TechMeld (where bots remained individual thinkers but are linked to share thoughts) was to advise and be the information source on human behaviour, human war and conflict and its aftermath. He had read 'Decline and Fall of the Roman Empire' and 'Decline of the West', and felt he had significant insights into how the human race had consistently overreached its ability to manage conflict and, after a War, how a political vacuum caused instability and turmoil. The tiny surviving population on this small island, a microcosm of the human race, desperately needed help if they were to survive into another generation. The survivors were in denial of their future: they had been either geared up for fighting or passively waiting to have their lives re-instated again. This remaining population didn't realise how difficult it was going to be for them to take over the essential work that the human race needed to survive long term. He suggested setting up a training programme. Plan A

A few weeks later Major Sperling called a confidential meeting with Sergeant Howard, the Military Surgeon Captain Khan and Julius. Major Sperling opened the meeting…..

"We are aware that a small group of islanders are challenging us by disabling the ancillary bots because they know we can repair them. It's clear that the Island population is totally unprepared to take on responsibilities for their own future. They seemed to be expecting us (I use the term collectively to include both military and bots) to run their lives for them whilst they grumble and blame us for the War. What was the result of Plan A Julius?"

Julius had set up two learning stations in the island's school house, the secondary Island Node linked to MAIN's IntraNet, and prepared to support students. He asked both groups of the island population for those with knowledge and practical skills to help in re-training. The response was underwhelming, but the recruitment of potential students far outstripped this in underwhelmingness, (Julius was a little uncertain of the grammar- perhaps it should be instripped?), but he knew what he meant.

"Now it's time for Plan B." said Major Sperllng. "I need an update on military and ancillary bot fitness and the progress of the TechMeld project."

Chapter Four

Marcus Stanley, a qualified electrician, volunteered for the Engineers at the first whispers of war, and landed at the island looking for excitement. With only basic training Marcus's War service to date consisted of wearing a uniform, counting the supplies in the warehouse, loading missiles into the four firing tubes and honing his technique in extreme nosiness linked to selective lightfingeredness. If asked to justify this Marcus would have called it 'providential curiosity'.

After the War he was tasked with collecting and repairing broken down ancillary bots and servicing the three electric CareCars, which involved him trailing about in the frequent rain and always cold. He found this not only uncomfortable, but also an insult to his management potential, and cut down his ability to carry on profitable arrangements with the islanders.

Marcus then volunteered to help in the hospital, providentially near to the stores. The ward was full of former combatants with healing wounds, or waiting for fitting of prosthetic limbs or further skin grafts. After a week working as an orderly the inmates requested that Marcus be found another job to volunteer for, as they were fed up of his looks of revulsion – and even worse – pity, when he looked at them. Mind you, Marcus was irritated and didn't see anything funny in the way his fellow soldiers would hoot when he walked in the ward.

"Watch out! Keep your hands on your wallets! Marcus has arrived!"

During his week in the hospital, he nosied around looking for stuff he could use as leverage to embarrass the bots or barter with the villagers. In a side ward he found five beds containing victims of the SonicFlash: three of them so badly burnt they would need years of skin grafts, but they were not expected to survive. One of the others, Mavis, had put her hands over her face when she heard the boom, and protected her eyes from the flash, but it burnt her hands, which were now covered with a metallic film. The fourth victim, Hanne, a Sergeant Engineer, had been looking out of the observation window and the flash burnt her upper body and hair. She had been fitted with a metal mesh skullcap, and her face, arms and chest had been sprayed with some sort of plastic skin which was cracking as it hardened.

Marcus asked one of the soldiers in the rehab ward, "What's that mesh on Hanne's head for?"

"It must be to calm her down," answered Joe, who was fitted with a faceplate and two new arms fixed to a breastplate, which also had connections for his amazing prosthetic legs.

"Without the cap on she kept hallucinating, shouting about strange events or asking if we saw things she says are going to happen in the future. She seemed to be in terrible pain. It was as exhausting for her as it was for us. It really upset Jacob, didn't it J?"

Jacob, (who was fitted with a bionic eye and ear attached to a metal cap protecting the injury to his skull) answered, "Before the War Hanne and I were an item, but we had to put that on hold. I couldn't bear to hear her shouting – and the thought of her waking up to see me like this made everything worse."

Marcus called several times over the next few weeks and noticed all the soldiers had been discharged, except for Joe and Jacob waiting for rehabilitation. Hanne and Mavis were still being kept under sedation so their bodies could heal. One day he found the side ward empty, and was told Hanne and Mavis had been moved somewhere quieter. Marcus went to visit Julius and asked him what the Carebots were doing to Hanne and Mavis.

"It seems that the SonicFlash rattled human brains, "said Julius. "The MAIN thinks that the Flash might have triggered some sort of telepathy in these two survivors. As this is on a 'non perceived frequency' it wanted to understand and monitor them as they recover."

This information about Hanne's behaviour troubled Marcus. It was a bit of a problem, but if he could just find her it could bring him a big step nearer his aim for a bot-free island with himself voted in charge by grateful islanders.

Chapter Five

Island Headteacher Victoria Szabbo's degree was in Classics, (her area of expertise was Ancient Rome, though her Latin was dodgy). She had remained quiet and inconspicuous for a year after the military arrival at the island, hoping no one would notice the number of school pupils attending out of a possible 11 varied between 5 and zero, most days zero. Victoria had been delighted when Julius confessed his name was due to his interest in the Roman Empire.

She was then even more pleasantly surprised when Julius asked her to help with his project to train islanders, because he thought that having her help would encourage islanders to come forward. But the Islanders thought she was chosen because she would say 'Yes' to everything. And she did. Not just 'Yes' to anything but 'Oh Julius! What a good idea' to everything. But two-faced worms can turn eventually. True, it had taken her a week or so of agonising to bring her to the final decision to act but it really had to be today. Victoria had joined MOBO (Military Out Bots Out) over a year ago, because she was mesmerised by the handsome Marcus and thought he was brilliant. Her role in MOBO was to recruit members, and she was doing really well. The islanders wanted rid of the military and the bots (but we can keep the Carebots can't we? Oh Yes, of course!).

Victoria aimed a seemingly casual kick at the panelling hiding the Server in her office. The thin wood rattled. Classic's specialist Victoria was imagining the server node as a box containing a robot head with wires sprouting from it like Medusa. Marcus had told her that there would be screws somewhere at the edges holding the cover on. There they were, six of them. She was about to get her nail file out of her pocket to have a go at unscrewing them, when she heard a familiar clumping on the corridor outside. It was not a good time for a visit, he was impossible to get rid of quickly.

"Good Day, Senior Techbot of the Learning Service," Victoria greeted her visitor. Attired in his long black tailcoat (to make him more accessible to humans) he looked almost the same strange weirdo he always did, but Victoria could sense something was very wrong. His tailcoat had a spare button at the top and extra buttonhole at the bottom.

"Victoria, you know you can call me Julius when there is no one else here," the large bot replied. "I am very worried, and need your human advice."

"I'm sorry, Julius," said Victoria, "I'm very busy just now."

They both looked at her desk, which had just one paper on it.

"I think you can leave the monthly report on the three possible student enrolments for a little while," Julius said, and Victoria was reminded, yet again, it was dangerous to treat bots like fools, even if they looked it.

Julius sat himself in her comfy chair, leaving Victoria to sit in the hard visitor's chair. What could she do now? She couldn't say she was ill or he would ship in a CareBot to give her half an aspirin.

"Of course, I have a large pile of other work to get through this week," Victoria said, showing an impressive pile of papers in her briefcase, and hoping Julius couldn't spot that there were several knitting patterns (once she learnt how to spin the sheep fleece she could begin to knit again). There were also lists of ideas for games for the Winter Solstice party (Julius was politely ambivalent on this way to get bots and humans to connect, never mind the military and islanders).

"I don't want to stop you working, Victoria, but things appear to be getting out of hand. I have been in total agreement of the MAIN's policies to support humans, caring for them, protecting and teaching them. But I am concerned about the direction of developments."

"Do you mean the recent restriction of islander access and deletion of the social media Instanote and Friendlyspace on the

IntraNET?" said Victoria, thinking this could be a chink in the armour.

"Oh No," said Julius, "I totally agree that all that conflict and spite against other humans was harmful psychologically – and, in fact, I recommended the policy to MAIN. And, of course, the islanders have access to the resources of DataWeb held on our servers for study and interest.

"So, what's the issue?" said Victoria.

"There are two problems," said Julius, "Firstly, I'm worried about longer term food shortages for humans on this island. There seems to be a delusion that in the near future imports to the island will start again."

Julius explained that fresh food stocks were getting depleted as there were not enough humans willing to work in the fields. One or two crofters were managing their own smallholdings but were unwilling to share their winter-storage surplus. Already root vegetables were rotting in the ground and fruit was not being picked.

"But Julius," said Victoria, "Why can't the bots just do the work in the fields?"

"For three reasons," said Julius, "Firstly the islanders keep disabling and breaking ancillary bots, secondly, the wet and dirt make our joints seize up, but mainly because our role here is to support recovery and independence, not live human's lives for them."

"Oh! Yes, I see," said Victoria, thinking it would be easy enough to waterproof bots if they wanted to.

"I can see that's a worry," she said, "But I don't think I can help. What else were you concerned about?"

"I believe that things have gone a step too far. Last week you may have noticed that there was another demonstration outside the military base, by people who were refusing to take up essential roles in return for getting their food provided."

"Yes, I noticed, but they had dispersed a day later, I assumed they were fine with their arrangements." said Victoria.

"These humans appear to have now vanished. I think they could have been removed against their will into the cavern under the mountain. I have always believed our purpose here is to care for and support humans but I don't agree with undue coercion," said Julius. "Another thing I should mention, Marcus came to me and asked about a missing person, and I was able to find out that she was part of a monitoring experiment being undertaken remotely by MAIN, and told him where she was. That was just an understandable misunderstanding, but this is unacceptable."

"Haven't you heard anything from the other Techbots?" asked Victoria.

<<JuliusMELDQuery I am concerned about the recent disappearance of humans. What information have you about this?>>

<<MELDresponse Humans are in the cavern under the mountain. We believe that this was at the direct order of the MAIN. The reason appears to be the necessity for organising islander transport>>

"Our Techmeld is not linked to the Intranet or the military and we don't have direct access to MAIN , which operates independently from military and bots. But there is a suggestion this is connected with something called 'Islander Transports' which sounds suspiciously like duress to me."

"Julius, my friend, I believe you are a good person, and only someone in your situation can protest about this. Can't you contact MAIN and ask for clarification because you are concerned?" said Victoria.

"You're right, Victoria. I will do it now."

Julius put his finger in the socket next to the Learning Node cover. Less than a minute later he fell over, deactivated, his finger still stuck in the port.

Victoria was stunned, though probably not entirely surprised. Luckily Julius had fused the Node and done the work for Marcus for her.

Up to you now Marcus, thought Victoria. The euphoria soon evaporated as she realised she had to leave poor Julius here on her office floor and stride over him all day. She decided she needed to contact Marcus somehow.

Chapter Six

Mavis can see the figure staggering slowly up the hill has now stopped. She's a strange sight - dressed in large overalls with sleeves hanging down over her hands, and the trousers wrinkled up to her knees. Suddenly she falls forward on her face. Mavis gingerly shuffles down to help, frightened of slipping down the hillside. As she reaches the woman, she notices her sprutty hair is poking through a shiny metal net skullcap. She turns her head and speaks to Mavis.

"Everyone's gone!" she says, "Can't you hear the loudspeaker?"

"Sorry, love," replies Mavis, "I'm really deaf. Come on see if you can stand up."

There is no way the woman can stand. They manage to struggle her round and get her sitting up.

"What's your name?" asked Mavis. "I can't recognise you with all that stuff covering your face."

"I don't know," answered the woman. "I don't remember an effing thing until I woke up in that room an hour ago. Can you see the sky ladders?"

"Where?" asked Mavis.

"Down there, at the edge of the shore in the distance."

"Sorry," said Mavis. "I've not got my glasses with me. I'm as blind as a bat."

"Bats aren't blind, they 'see' by echolocation using ultrasonic waves."

"Well, you haven't forgotten everything have you?" said Mavis. "You must be a scientist."

"I think I used to be," said the mystery woman.

"We need help," said Mavis. "Where are the CareBots when you need them?"

As she spoke, they saw a CareCar making its way up the hill. It stopped near them and Ajax jumped out and ran over.

"I spoke too soon," said Mavis. "Here's a CareBot – how on earth did he know we were here?"

"I told him," said Marcus following Ajax out of the car.

Ajax and Marcus helped both women into the vehicle, and Ajax gave them both a nutribar and a vitdrink. Mavis was annoyed.

"What are you waiting for? We are both ill and need hospital care, she has lost her memory and doesn't know who she is, and I need these things taking from my hands," she said.

"Who do you think put them onto your hands?" answered Ajax. "And the hospital ward is now closed because the remaining Carebots and other ancillary bots have been damaged and withdrawn. I can help but you will have to wait."

"Hurry," said Marcus, "We have very little time."

Marcus realised he needed to get Hanne onto his side, but unless she got her memory back she was going to be no help at all.

"Hanne, I am so sorry. How are you feeling?"

"I feel as if I'm going mad. I need you to listen and tell me you hear the loudspeaker."

They all listened and after a minute she heard a faint loudspeaker announcement. 'Come to your Embarkation Point.' Only Hanne heard it, though Marcus nodded in a non-committal kind of way as though he may have heard.

"Now," said Hanne, "Tell me you can see the skyladders on the shore.

Ajax replied truthfully, "No, I can't see them,"

Hanne said "I suppose it could have been another time. The metal on my head must have scrambled time. Because if I blink, I can also see that there are no skyladders there now, but if I close my eyes, I can see people going up the skyladders."

Marcus groaned. "I'm sorry, we have no time to find out why you are seeing this. We are all going to be in trouble if we stay here and the Network reconnects."

Both women demanded that the metal was removed from their bodies first.

Ajax brought some medical tools in his Carekit and then gently snipped off the net on Hanne's head bit by bit, as Marcus cut the 'gauntlets' off Mavis's hands. Hanne's head and Mavis's hands were sore and bleeding after the removal, pinpricks of blood showing where the mechanisms had penetrated the skin. Ajax dabbed them clean with cloths from his medipack, and sprayed a protective coating to cover the skin whilst it healed, and wrapped soft bandages around Hanne's arms where the skin was peeling. With the net off her head, Hanne was recovering her memory.

Whilst they had some food and drink the women chatted in low voices. It was a stupid move, Marcus now knew, to move both women and let them exchange views. He wished he hadn't taken the trouble to find them, trundle both women on a trolley, one by one, down the tunnels into the empty missile silos. AND then go back and set the outer doors to open, and lights come on when Victoria fused the circuit. They weren't going to be grateful and do what he wanted were they?

"Marcus," said Mavis, "I don't agree with MOBO. I'm not helping you, so please take me back to the pub!"

"Marcus," said Hanne. "Mavis tells me we've been sedated and unconscious for a long time. The unmonitored MAIN could decide to do any crazy thing it wants to without daily oversight. AND I need to see Jacob. The quickest way is to go back through the missile tunnels."

Ajax brought Hanne two crutches, and then drove Mavis in the vehicle down the hillside, setting off around the headland and onto the track to the pub.

Marcus, with Hanne on crutches, walked slowly back through the tunnels whilst he explained why he had 'saved' her and Mavis from the hidden observation ward.

"I need you to disable MAIN," said Marcus, "So the islanders can be free."

"MAIN should possibly have been disabled weeks ago." said Hanne, "but I need to check with the TechMeld to find out what has been happening."

Marcus could hardly believe things were going to work out OK for him, after all!

Chapter Seven

When Ajax crossed the island to take Mavis back to the pub, they saw a heap of clothes on the track ahead of them. Not clothes, but a man lying on his face. Ajax stopped and got out, and saw it was the dead body of an islander. He could also see what looked like another body wearing bright clothes in the distance. Mavis had seen them too.

"That looks like Victoria, the School teacher." she said.

"I think I should take you to join the other islanders in the cave under the mountain before I go for a look," said Ajax. Mavis agreed.

At the military base.

"Extra hands needed working in the mountain," said Sergeant Howard, "We only just got the rest of the islanders to safety. MAIN informs us we need to arm the islanders and take as many ancillaries we can muster to protect them whilst we do so. Have we got the rest of the soldiers packed and ready to load up?"

The 'Cyborg Squad' as they started to call themselves, some 9 strong (and strong being the operative term for some of the metal-repaired men) lined up in the open mustering area next to the tunnel doors, having finished packing their equipment.

Just then Marcus arrived with Hanne slowly following behind.

"What's with all the shouting in the cave?" asked Marcus.

"Where have you been? Didn't you notice? The island is being invaded! There's a submarine surfaced in the sea behind the cliff, and enemy marines are ashore looking for food supplies and munitions." answered Sergeant Howard.

"Why don't you fire the missiles?" asked Marcus.

"They're facing the wrong way, and HQ have the codes."

"I can get the codes," said Hanne as she overhead the exchange.

Hanne made her way to the Techmeld's door and entered the key code. As the door swung open Marcus looked over her shoulder into the room, entirely dark except for four shadows and a series of blue lasers intersecting the darkness. The door closed and after a few minutes Hanne re-appeared.

"Who can fire the missiles?" she asked.

"I can," said Marcus. He went to the missile control panel at the side of the tunnel and opened it. Hanne input the code and Marcus asked, "Is it safe to fire?"

"Go with it," said Sergeant Howard.

The light on the control board turned green. After a few seconds there was a high-pitched whistling sound. Later they saw the vid of the first missile flying low out of the tunnel and turning sharp right. As it hit the submarine a huge waterspout shot up into the air and cascaded over the top of the cliff.

"Don't waste the other," said Captain Sperling, having entered the double doors to the base carrying Julius's feet whilst another two soldiers carried the rest of his body.

"The Techmeld told us they couldn't complete their work without their 5th member, and Julius was deactivated over in the school house. If we leave him here, he will re-boot soon."

The Captain did a double take, "Sergeant Stohl, how glad I am to see you're back with us."

"Thank God you're safe Hanne," Jacob heard the Captain, and rushed up to her.

"I'm surprised you recognised me," said Hanne, "though I could say the same about you."

"It would be a toss-up who would win the Ugliest Mug competition," said Joe coming up to hug her. "Cheeky bxgger! Listen who's talking," Hanne replied.

163

"Look, I need another urgent word with the Techmeld, about the MAIN," said Hanne, and disappeared again behind their door.

"Can you tell us exactly what is happening," Captain Sperling asked Hanne when she came out again.

"It's what I was frightened of, when it was decided to have only one human able to shut down MAIN. I understood it was for security reasons, but when I was injured, no-one human or bot could take over, even though the Techmeld knew everything that was happening."

"It seemed that the MAIN, on its own initiative, is acting as a powerful beacon, drawing in all kinds of crafts like moths to a flame. It is so powerful it could be drawing visitors to Earth from the centre of the galaxy, though the Earth will be gone if they ever arrive! But locally, as well as the enemy sub, the Techmeld have data on two further large sea-going vessels approaching. Long range observation shows one to be a cruise ship with thousands of refugees, far too many people for this small island to help. Techmeld tested their new instrument using it to remotely re-set the cruise ship's GPS to the nearest mainland with probable survivors. The other ship was showing 'friendly' identification, though it is technically possible that enemy fighters have commandeered it. This will arrive within 24 hours. Techmeld want the MAIN removed from the network and wired into an electronic transit box before any other craft arrived."

Jacob and Joe supported Hanne, whilst half the squad flanked her, and delivered her to the hatch protecting the MAIN. Her iris scan and fingerprint were needed to open the inner hatch cover, and then the mechanism was lifted out of its canister and put into the electronic transit box to be taken back to the Techmeld by the squad. Hanne then went as quickly as she could to find her clean clothes and fill her backpack.

Meanwhile the other half of the squad, battling the storm, had swept the island up to the town and found two enemy marines filling sacks with food at the shop. Also, as Ajax had

164

arrived back for Victoria, they helped the bot, who was in danger of fusing its electronics in the lightening and torrential rain, lift her into the CareCar.

Captain Sperling went into the open-fronted vaulted cave housing the islanders, they had lit fires and were sat around talking. It could almost look like they were having a picnic if they hadn't looked so miserable. There looked to be pitifully few islanders and soldiers compared with the numbers when they had arrived.

"I'm here to brief you on what has been happening," he said.

He explained about the invasion and how three enemy marines had been captured, though there had been no decision made as to what to do with them. He also told them about the 'friendly' ship which would be arriving the day after, and whose crew and passengers may well want to stay on the island for a while.

Captain Sperling also told them that the military had decided that, as they were still a combat unit, their responsibility was to continue reconnaissance and join with other groups of colleagues , so would be going back on duty and leaving in the needle crafts the same way they had arrived. They would leave during the night, leaving guns and ammunition for the islanders in case they found any more enemy marines hiding out. He wasn't going to advise them but, if they decided to stay on the island, they may be glad of additional fit men to help. There were also the landing crafts the enemy marines had arrived in which would get them to the mainland when they were ready.

"What about the stores?"

"We are sharing the stores. Marcus has volunteered to stay with you and help you with access to them - he tells me there are beer-making kits! He can also advise you on dealing with the prisoners, protecting the island, and training you on use of the firearms and any other military resources left on the island."

Marcus tried to look friendly and helpful rather than triumphant and excited. How he would have liked to shout, 'I'm in charge now!' Not, of course, understanding what a nightmare of a job this was going to be.

"What about the bots?"

Julius stepped forward and answered, "As you wanted, we will all be leaving."

Suddenly it seemed to go deadly quiet, the sound of the storm muffled.

Chapter Eight

With the storm still raging the islanders decided to stay in the cave until the morning. The military packed their gear, supplies and ancillary bots into the needle boats, and settled down for a couple of hours sleep before departing. The Techmeld cleared their laboratory and packed boxes ready to leave.

At midnight a lookout came into the base to wake them up.

"There's something in the sky above the island."

Most of the squad came out into the open and looked up.

In spite of the heavy rain and wind, the enormous whale-shaped craft held quite steady high above the island. It was difficult to see very clearly with the cloud cover, but two doors opened in the side with huge search lights illuminating the ground. Then the sky ladders were released onto the shore.

This time everyone heard the loudspeaker.

"Come immediately to your Embarkation Point."

The five Techmeld, carrying the boxes with their PNTimeSlide optical device and the NodeBrain walked towards the airship.

Hanne had known this time was coming ever since she woke up in the tunnel and walked out with her backpack.

"Come on with me to Marsbase," she shouted to Jacob and her 'Cyborg squad' colleagues, "With the new Timesliding Tech we may get to the stars!"

And three humans and five bots got onto the sky ladders and were pulled into the ship. Then blink! It was gone.

Did Stannkenstein Finally Discover Transmutation?

Chapter One
ONEDAY

0833 Earth Standard Time (EST): Near Earth Monitoring Station

Earth is almost a no fly zone for spacecraft – only armoured craft make it through the debris field which in practice means monthly visits of the Lunar ferry, Mars mining craft once or twice a year and the N.E.M. Station's annual return trip.

Several arks of the exodus of the fourth millennium fled the encroaching ice and then returned as twisted wreckage spat out from the node portal and exacerbated an already critical problem. After centuries of investigation astrophysicists are still unable to discover the quantum rules that determine why this stellar waystation transmits matter in only one direction.

Sky Sweeping duties on the Near Earth Monitoring Station, orbiting in the packed graveyard of four millennia of space junk surrounding the earth, have only rare moments of drama. Operating the long grapple to snare lumps of obsolete comms and spacecraft stuff and then truss it onto one of the re-entry drones offers only 30 minutes or so of aerobic exercise. Using the magnetic ionised paddles to catch the lethal micro particles and then whack them into the atmosphere to burn up was routine. The only really stressful time is at changeover.

The message ping arrived just as the (sole) Duty Officer of the Near Earth Monitoring Station watched his shift relief miss the docking port for the third time. After a year's duty his patience was as thin as his muscle mass so the message arrival triggered not just the alarm but also an apoplectic episode. Hence the considerably delayed ongoing transmission to SpacePort City.

After his extended stay at the therapeutic facility Commander Enth of the Earth Space Police felt positive and more relaxed then he had for years. His barely contained quadripolar disorder had been budding off tiny phobias every month until he could no longer get a grip. His Duty Officer told him to go and get it sorted. The treatment had been BrainWave technology that pulled together his wonky brain scaffolding.

After the treatment the Doctor told Enth:

"I've fitted a neuroprothesis into your pre-frontal lobe which fixes the unstable gene template. It stops any adrenaline and other stress chemical build up and manages your neurotransmitters. From now on work stress will act to energise your brain and trigger hyperthinking. But remember, if your brain becomes overstimulated and the mechanism overheats, it will temporarily turn you off."

And here he was having walked under the vault of the high grey sky without agoraphobia, no finger agnosia, no nose dysmorphia whilst looking at his reflection in the mirror this morning, no feelings of anxiety. Wonderful. All gone. But. Lurking in there somewhere was an uneasy feeling that the problem with Lalli Mak was not entirely resolved.

0855 EST Skyport Space Hub. Enth's Office

The current trickle of space traffic needed only a skeleton staff, and the Space Comms Centre was pretty deserted as usual. Duty Officer Erl Trant, ex Luna ferry pilot would be supervising customs at Skyport Launch slings. Investigator Lalli Mak, set on by the Governor to at least quadruple freight traffic into earth by finding clearways through the debris field, would have already completed the daily scan and be looking around to interfere with something else. Condescending polymath Mak would soon be arriving as usual: ' I'll organise that for you, Let me do the rota, sort that for you in no time....'

Arriving in his office Commander Enth checked his comms screen and found all the day's tasks completed. Rats. She had been around already. Still, after the disturbance of his treatment he could now take time to polish his console. Take a break.

0925 EST Skyport Space Hub Admin Centre

The message bleep from the Near Earth Monitoring station arrived. The Duty Surveillance Officer hot-potatoed the transmission to Commander Enth. In the quiet of his office the siren was a heart-stopping shock. An inadvertent inhalation of his faux blueberry and turnip lunch bar led to dribbles of slightly corrosive fluorescent blue fluid down the front of his best uniform. Just now he was as irritated by the spreading purple blob on his suit as the flashing alarm. He closed his eyes: the irritation faded.

Then he read the message:

<<NEM STATION REPORT SIGNAL FROM OUTSIDE SOLAR SYSTEM THEY THINK FROM ALIEN CRAFT. ADVISE URGENTLY ON ACTION. >>

His brain was suddenly clear, sharp and organised: he replied:

<<AMBER SECURITY LOCKDOWN CODE 4. NO EXTERNAL COMMUNICATIONS EXCEPT THROUGH MY OFFICE. SPACE INCIDENT INVESTIGATOR AND ASTROTECH STAFF IDENTIFY THE CRAFT & ITS POSITION. MEETING 1030 ALL SECURITY STAFF>>

Focussed and speed thinking, Commander Enth made a list of all 18 items of information he needed to solve the mystery of the so-called alien craft and prioritised them in importance. Investigator Lalli Mak and AstroTechnician Hasser sent him the information he asked for within 10 minutes.

174

Two ticks on his list.

1030 EST. Meeting in Skyport Space Comms Centre

Luckily by the meeting time the big purple stain on Commander Enth's warm suit had crept down off the nanoprotective coating and was left behind temporarily on his boot. He confidently faced his Space Security Communications staff and summarised the current position: a transmission had been received by the Near Earth Monitoring Station and forwarded to this team.

AstroTechnician Hasser's researchers found that the transmission was activated by earth frequency codes. These had been emitted by a spacecraft passing OUT of the local node portal. Investigator Lalli Mak found the codes in the archive belonging to a ship owned by an ore miner called Norris.

Enth concluded "Why and how this ore miner's ship came OUT of the IN star portal 12 years after he set off supposedly going to the asteroid belt we may never find out. The most urgent questions come first: AstroTechnician Hasser find out how long we have before this spacecraft arrives in the solar system. Investigator Mak see if you can track down Norris. Comms Officer Claddis find out about availability of spacecraft and defensive missiles and see the Tech Unit forwards the ship's transmissions as soon as they are decoded. Finally, team, if anything filters out to the media and leads to unrest, in fact, if there is even a whisper, anyone involved will be put into deep freeze. Is that clear?"

As the team left Lalli Mak stayed behind and approached Enth, who tried to keep his face averted and pretend she wasn't there. Not to be put off, Investigator Mak cleared her throat.

"I don't think that an ore miner like Norris was leading this expedition. My time would be better spent looking for a likely candidate. I reckon that the overall leader of this expedition is a scientist and has access to considerable backing to fund a stellar voyage. Also, he or she must have been missing for 12 years at least. I'll contact the Records Officer at Skyport Academy to see if they can identify any scientists with this description."

After she went Commander Enth was frustrated that Lalli Mak had struck again, but mainly he was annoyed that he hadn't had the idea first. Later his wrist comm signalled several messages:

Digicom from Astrotechnician Hasser

<<Having measured the current speed and velocity of the spacecraft of interest, based on a comparison to its original estimated position on node exit, I calculate that it is already within the solar system and if the current trajectory is maintained will reach the orbit of Mars in 7 days.>>

Digicom from Comms Officer Claddis: Information as requested

<<There are two Space Police Cruisers in hangars at Luna City and one on Mars Base. All are operational but only one of the lunar craft is ready and armed. The others could be fitted with missiles with a range of warheads within two days, though there are none present on Mars and only limited stores on the Moon. To have a full range of warheads available on both sites would take up to eight days. Or it is possible to hire space craft and missiles immediately from the MarsOreMining Inc on Mars>>

With this new information Enth contacted the Mars Colony Space Police Commander to get things moving to intercept the ship.

Message reads as follows:

<<SHIP WITH TRAJECTORY INTERSECTING YOUR SPACE AFTER EXITING LOCAL NODE PORTAL DUE 7 DAYS. EARTH REGISTERED SHIP LEFT EARTH 12 YEARS AGO. CAPTAIN CALLED NORRIS. UNKNOWN CREW. UNKNOWN BUT POSSIBLY HIGHLY VALUAB LE CARGO. PREPARE TO INTERCEPT OR DESTROY. ERECT TEMPORARY DOME IN NON-TERRAFORMED AREA AND HIRE ARMED SPACECRAFT FROM MARSOREMINING INC. CONTACT SHIP'S A1 TO ORDER LANDING AS YOUR INSTRUCTION. SHIP IDENTIFICATION CODES FOLLOW>>

Enth thought it was a clever plan to mention the possibility of a valuable cargo. That should stop the trigger-happy Mars crew blasting the ship out of the sky with little or no provocation.

14.45 Voice message from Lalli Mak to Commander Enth

"Expedition Leader identified by Skyport Academy most likely as Professor Stann Bistort, suspended 14 years ago from the Academy for causing an explosion. He always was a recluse and no one has seen him since his expulsion. Stann Bistort's father was Edween Bistort, Mining Billionaire. This one fits the profile. I've asked for information to be sent to you.

<>

Enth studied Norris's log record written on the third day after setting off from Luna 12 years ago. Now he had information for three more of his list items, he confirmed the name of the survey leader, found the name of the planet and one of the purposes of the survey, but what was really interesting he had to add two more items to investigate onto his list. He then contacted Lalli Mak.

2000 Mem to Lalli Mak

<< Good work identifying Stann Bistort. Read Norris's Log account. Meeting Twoday 13.00. >>

Reply<<Confirm meeting 1300. I'll bring my notes>>

Then he wrote his report to the Governor.

Chapter Two

TWODAY

10.00 EST Sky City Council Offices Suite: Visit of Enth to Governor Washh

Commander Enth had to brief the SkyCity Governor on the situation, and do so in such a way to prevent any unnecessary impulsive action. He set off from his office in Skyport to slide the corridor into SkyCity and the Council Chamber.

Meanwhile, Governor Washh was not just annoyed, he was very cross indeed. With his ministers he had just had three days of trying to judge the entries to the prestigious Energy Tech Award – the quinquennial energy saving competition. The entries varied from the absolutely ridiculous to the simply stupid. His minister's comments varied from the absolutely stupid to the simply ridiculous.

What do you do with people who are unaware that proposals to "cut energy to old people" or "reducing the energy supply to 10% of food plexipods" were not technical solutions as specified in the Award guidelines? Not a brain cell between them. Governor Washh moved up from furious to being incandescent with rage. Under missile fire from desk ornaments placed for the purpose, his ministers retreated. Washh retrieved his large blue ExtraGel Ice Cap and stuck it on his head. Breathe. Calm.

Governor Washh was waiting for Commander Enth when he arrived. Enth was about to launch into his announcement when Governor Washh held up his hand to quieten him.

"I was wondering when you were going to bother to come and tell me. You first need to know that I have instructed Space Police Commander Jaste at Mars Base to contact the ship and if the response is unsatisfactory, prepare to intercept and destroy it"

Commander Enth tried not to stare at the thing on Governor Washh's head whilst he processed the meaning of his words. "Why have you done that?" he asked, voice rising an octave.

"Because, you would dither over the decision. The ship is due in six days, and this is about protecting the Earth from threat, and I can't let you dither with that" replied Washh.

"I am working quickly" Enth replied, "I have systematically analysed the situation and have a list of 20 items needed to work out the level of risk. After only one day, I have all or partial information on 10 of them already. I think that is pretty efficient".

"Look Enth it's also only a day since you had your brain re-set and neuroprothesis fitted, and you are not stable enough to trust with this decision"

"How do you know about the implant in my head?" asked Enth.

"I heard you were sliding towards meltdown so I told Erl Trant, your Duty Officer to send you for help," answered Washh, "There's no disgrace in this: the human genome is now so fragmented that only a fraction of the population—the key competents like you and me-- can function in any task requiring persistence or independent thinking. Unfortunately the genes for intelligence are now inextricably linked to mental instability and severe introversion, and, as you must have noticed, to low libido. The nearer to genius, the worse the problem. You and I are mid-ways and are fixable. However, some of us do have a short fuse. (Washh gesticulated at the ice cap on his head.) By the way, your neuroprothesis: clever as it is, can't protect you from overload when people crowd your personal space which, in our case, is around a metre and a half."

Commander Enth took a moment or so to digest this information. "But you do admit that I am fixed now. I am very confident that the talented Investigator Mak and I can quickly solve the dilemma of whether and when to destroy the ship. Remember, it has returned to Earth through what we thought of as a one-way OUT portal. In addition to this the expedition was to mine rare substances from this planet, Verdant 3. There is so much to lose by just blowing it up."

Governor Washh thought for a while. " Well, this is the proverbial pandora's can of worms," he said quietly, " On the one hand we have evidence that the space node CAN be traversed in both directions and on the other some dangerous alien plague could be on its way to infect earth. So you better tell me what information you have."

Commander Enth concentrated on the latest information from Norris's Captain's log.

"Norris's log says that this ship, now called the 'Alchemist' was on its way to a 'green possibly wooded' planet called Verdant 3, in 61 Virginis. The expedition leader we know now was Stann Bistort who hired Norris, an ore miner, and three other crew and was expecting to stay only three days on the planet surface. All staff had been given their tasks: Rolly, the First Officer was to pilot the craft in orbit, Captain Norris and the exogeologist Baris were to excavate and fill the ore carrier trailer with rare minerals, on a profit-sharing basis. Wendo, the chemist was told that there were no living things on Verdant 3 and she was to examine planetary structures. Norris's log mentions him checking the heat shields on the landing suits as Stann said to expect high temperatures and superheated steam especially if they were near volcanic activity. The fact that this spacecraft has now returned suggests to me that some or all of the mission was successful and we have much to learn from this survey. There are two further important points arising from the Captain's report. Firstly, the ship was following what he called a 'photon trace' as a waymarker for navigation through the node portal and onward to Verdant 3 in 61 Virginis, and secondly he said that Stann had ordered the ship's A1 to have a limiter fitted, so it could not override his instructions."

He added: "When I analyse the next transmission I should be able to give a definite recommendation for the fate of the Alchemist."

Governor Washh decided. "I'll hold up Jaste on Mars for 30 hours. After that he will have the authority to make the final judgement".

When Commander Enth returned to his office, a message was waiting on his wrist comms.

Voice Message for Commander Enth and Investigator Mak from Space Academy Vice Chancellor:

"Information on Stann Bistort as requested. Stann was one of twins born to Edween Bistort the Mining Billionaire.

He was born blind and fitted with bionic eyes but no prosthetics could mend his psyche. Stann is a genius but a recluse, locked into himself and phobic with face to face contact. His knowledge and expertise in all branches of physics and astronomy - astrophysics, particle physics, mathematics, was already greater than all scientists at the academy by the time he was 12. It was said that his bionic eyes allowed him to 'see' across a huge range of bandwidths – and that he could 'see' subatomic particles. All kinds of myths like this grew around him and students nicknamed him 'Stannkenstein' after the mythical cyborg. The Academy created him a Professor which gave him access to Academy resources and in return he allowed students to share his data. The Academy was allowed to publish his work and patent his inventions as long as there was no attempt to use his name. I have tracked down five major projects developed by Stann though assigned to others at the time

Firstly, Stann Bistort always kept up to date with research in prosthetics and robotics. Secondly, the Annual Energy prize of 5125 was won by his invention of food plexipods that synthesized some amino acids and carbs from waste stuff nobody wants to know about.

183

Thirdly early in his career Stann Bistort started a very specialised and detailed scan of the underlying structure of the universe. He identified a space-time anomaly which know now accounts for the local node- the doorway to the stars found in the third millennium and used by survey vessels and arks for a time, even though no return gates have ever been identified. His students continued this work and many further OUT anomalies have been charted. It is said that Stann himself had developed a detailed network map of what he called 'space corridors'.

Fourthly, we know Stann Bistort had a particular interest in transmutation and had one of his students monitoring a planet in 61 Virginis to focus on an irregularity he had observed in spectra which he called 'systematic instability'.

Finally, Stann asked for Academy references to buy a powerful laser for a particular astrophysical experiment. He fired this massive laser which used around 4 quadrillion watts of power and fused all the electricity grid of the entire Skyport and Skycity area because he ran for more than the agreed 3 pico seconds. Professor Bistort was suspended from the Academy for two years, and soon after he dropped out of sight, and from then we have had no further contact with him. If you need more can I suggest you contact Professor Bistort's niece, Dr Sanda Bistort who is a physicist at the Academy"

Commander Enth forwarded the message to Lalli Mak, and ticked further items on his list and annotated others.

13.00 EST Meeting of Commander Enth with Investigator Mak

"We have only 25 hours to solve the problem of the Spaceship Alchemist." said Enth when Mak arrived "To save time we must analyse independently. You take information to date and I'll look at the next decoded log entry. Meet back in here at 15.00"

When the meeting reconvened Enth turned his work

console round and put a chair at each side. About a metre and a half apart. Mak looked approvingly at the arrangement. She then gave her analysis.

"I started with four questions" said Mak. "Why did billionaire Bistort hire such an inexperienced crew and choose an ore miner Norris? Why were they going to Verdant 3? What was the A1 limiter for? And what on earth was a photon trace?"

Looking at her notes Mak answered her own questions "I think it's obvious that Stann Bistort was in charge of everything – he must have pre-set all the flight plans and instructions for the journey and the A1 limiter would be to ensure that Norris couldn't change anything. And that is why he chose Norris – because although he was an experienced pilot he wouldn't think that he and his ship were being used as cover for something more sinister. And the crew were inexperienced scientists hired from a lunar project, none of them would be knowledgeable enough to challenge Stann or understand him and his plans."

"I agree," Enth said," But why go to Verdant 3 in such secrecy?"

"I don't think we know enough yet to know why they were going, and I'm expecting any further messages to tell us, but, there is a hint I think in the information from the Vice Chancellor, who mentions Stann's interest in transmutation on Verdant 3. Perhaps he was going to try to find the 'Philosopher's Stone'. There could be a clue in the fact the ship was called "Alchemist" for the journey. It took considerable research in the preserved microfilm archive – the ancient medieval Alchemists looked for the Philosopher's stone to transmute lead to gold. He could have been trying to find a catalyst for transmutation."

Commander Enth was impressed at these ideas, though he did think there may be more to the journey than this to keep it such a secret. "So what do you think the photon trace was?"

"My working hypothesis is that the laser Stann fired which caused the explosion was pointed at Verdant 3 and left a trail of photons from here to the 61 Virginis system. It would also imply that Stann had devised some instrument to detect this trace and follow it as a guide."

"Excellent work, Investigator Mak," said a thoughtful Enth before continuing, "Now rather than me just reading through the next log record with my comments, I think time will be better spent if you continue your expert insightful analysis of planetfall whilst I make an urgent visit to Sanda Bistort."

Before he left Commander Enth said shyly, "By the way, Investigator Mak, I would be privileged to step aside and work for you as Assistant Commander."

Lalli Mak threw back her head and laughed, "Horace Enth, I don't want to be Commander. I am aiming to be the next Governor."

15.30 EST Digimessage to Investigator Mak: Analysis of Alchemist Log Recording

"Wendo's recording is made when she is back on the ship after a visit to the planet surface. Hers is the only description we will have of Verdant 3. She starts by saying what she can see from orbit and mentions 'red fire' which we can assume links to the volcanic nature of the planet mentioned in Norris's log."

'When we came out of stasis we were already in orbit around Verdant 3, it was showing thick greeny gray clouds with only glimpses of what could be vegetation covering the planet surface. As we orbited we could see red fire in patches.'

She mentions that they are affected by timelock stasis sickness and Rolly's lungs were affected and was put into the Autodoc (but obviously could still operate the ship controls as later information tells us). Wendo says that Stann was already in his suit and stacking his crates for transport and was ready to go when Wendo woke up. Norris, Wendo and Stann were to go first, with Norris and Wendo building the base storage from Autobuild kit and Stann going off to do his own work. They fixed the ore carrier to the Lander to transport to the surface and then set off.

On the way down Wendo noted:

'…my view was distorted by my face plate and the domed plex of the Lander. I barely noticed the cloud thinning as we sank slowly through the thick swirling clouds. We saw the green tops of enormously high trees masking the planet surface. As we got closer I realised that these were not trees at all. The 'branches' were a vast interlinking lattice of translucent green tubes which shattered as the lander touched them. We were creating our own extensive clearing to land in. The slanted shafts of sunlight from Verdant 3's red dwarf highlighted the high degree of axis tilt. The light strobed and flickered as we passed the thick green poles supporting the lattice framework. Nearer the surface we could see fumes escaping from cracks in the planet crust.'

So the initial view of Verdant 3 appears to confirm Stann's assertion that the 'vegetation' was not living matter, but a mineralized phenomenon. The high temperature of the planet does not come from radiant heat from the star – at this oblique angle there seemed to be only little light masked by the 'vegetation'.

'We climbed down onto the wet brown shale surface, with brown torrential rain flooding down on us, and then draining through the porous surface. We turned on the new Supaslide 'zero' friction nanocoating on our suits and the high-shine mirror surface it formed repelled the rain so it haloed our suits and left Norris and I free to do our set tasks of setting up the first base storage cabin and lab whilst Stann loaded his boxes on the hopper and set off. We lifted the ore carrier trailer off the Lander and set the Autobuild in process. Whilst we were waiting we walked along the pathway created by our landing, framed by the towering green tubes. We saw Stann in a small clearing already setting up his equipment and walked slowly past on the spongy surface to the 12 metre cliff formed by surface upheaval and slippage already pinpointed as a target for Baris. We could see the distinct striations of dull coloured mineral layers, unbelievably the lines seeming to be constantly slowly moving upwards whilst at the same time standing still in a rippling effect.

On our way back we saw Stann again who by this time had set up spotlights in the dim light, lighting a hologram of a young girl. This was surrounded by a number of objects that were already sinking into the surface.'

Stann shows little interest in what his team members are doing, and has not disclosed to them what he intends to do. It is not clear what the setting up of the hologram is for. Is this communication with the planet? Also, the apparent movement of the layers in the upraised cliff seen by Norris and Wendo is possibly the evidence for transmutation seen in the planet spectra by Stann when observing from earth. Wendo continues.

'When we returned the cabin was complete and we set up the Chem Lab ready for use. Norris set off back to the ship to pick up Baris. I had my first scientific analysis to undertake. I walked over to the nearest green pole sinking each step into the spongy surface around the 'trunk'. The external shell, the 'trunk' of the growths themselves seemed to be some kind of constant mineral extrusion from Verdant 3's crust. It was crystalline, hollow, and quite brittle and whilst I was stood there a 'branch' fell to the ground onto my foot. The shearing of the 'branch' appeared to be caused when the extrusion was in process. I carefully broke off a small side offshoot stood back and managed to avoid the brown superheated viscous fluid spurting out. At the same time I could see the 'buds' of new 'trunks' pushing out from the ground. The cuticle, though eventually brittle, must be initially flexible, and strong to withstand the high turgor pressure and temperature.

When it cooled a little I took substantial samples of the gel and broken cuticle plus a piece of shale from the surface, for analysis in the Chem Lab. Used to working in a suit doing this stuff on Luna, it was a quick initial scan of the material. There was no sign of any cell structure or inclusions and the spectral investigation anomalous – each test a different answer. Was this an example of the transmutation Stann expected to find?'

Wendo here confirms the outgrowths on the planet surface are mineralised extrusions from the hot and highly pressurised planet interior. Does this whole edifice of pseudo trunks and branches have a specific function? The brittle cuticle must have been particularly sharp, because Wendo then notices her face plate fogging because of a suit leak and Norris took her back to the Alchemist leaving Baris to excavate the ore.

<<Note to Lalli Mak: Please check my analysis and add to my notes. Meeting at 900 tomorrow. We are fast running out of time so I'll look through the final log account when the decoding is complete.>>

1830 EST Visit of Enth to see Dr Sanda Bistort at Bistort Towers

Commander Enth decided to walk the short distance to Bistort Towers. He stepped out of the door into the usual early evening intense cold. At minus 80 degrees the cloud of his breath froze and fluttered to the ground in a sparkly shower with a Sssshh. Not good to stand still in this temperature he walked as quickly as he could cracking and popping on the ice-shelled snow path..

Lucky that Commander Enth wasn't eating a lunch bar when he saw Sanda Bistort for the first time. The door was opened by an android who tried unsuccessfully to wrestle his bag from him. He was shown into a large room and confronted by a woman who was wearing a thin red dress and no warm suit. Shock. Then the heat in the room hit him like a wave and he felt himself begin to faint. He pushed the android away when it attempted to unfasten his warmsuit.

"You won't need that suit in Bistort Towers" said a voice, "we can afford the energy bills to keep the house warm all the time."

Commander Enth looked at the amused face of Sanda Bistort. Keeping his dignity with difficulty he reached into his bag and put on his Blue ExtraGel Ice Cap. He could swear the android was smirking.

189

"Well, you want to know about Professor Stann Bistort, I believe" Sanda said, not at all fazed, whisking across the room. Enth fended her off with a stiff arm and moved his seat. This was no time discover whether he had hormones or not. He briefly summarised the situation and the information he hoped she could help with. He switched on his comms to record.

"Actually," said Sandra Bistort," I'm Stann's cousin, not niece. My father was Edween Bistort's brother. I'm 15 years younger than Stann and his twin sister Nessi.

I believe that Stann worked here in his laboratory with two students using the Space Academy's equipment, monitoring Verdant 3. He decided that they were seeing evidence of systematic particle instability. The particles, you know, fermions and bosons and all the esoteric stuff? (Nod Nod) Not expelled from the atoms as in radioactivity but this was transmutation, a pulsing change from one configuration to another in the same space. His collaborators believed that Stann thought that the changes were being triggered by something. He conjectured that if he could get a powerful enough laser to project a narrow beam of light onto Verdant 3 he could illuminate the key areas and answer some of his questions. You've heard of the Laser explosion? (Nod) Well, Stann wasn't prepared for the personal blowback – the explosion and outage killed Nessi's pet parrot and she was devastated. She committed suicide several weeks later, but it may not have been directly related.

Stann was suspended from the Academy for two years, but he was devastated about Nessi's death and built a little shrine to her with a holo, her ashes and a number of her personal possessions, flowers, little toys and the embalmed parrot. My mother showed me a vidcam image of it. Gruesome.

Stann had to cut off contact with Academy students after his expulsion. However, his disappearance was finally confirmed by his legal representatives and I was given authority to manage his assets in his absence. So I moved here from MedCity 4 years ago. Until you told me I had no idea that there was any expedition in process to Verdant 3. Actually I thought he could be staying in Bistort owned buildings off on a satellite or a Bistort mining colony."

"So did you personally know Stann and his sister Nessi?" queried Enth

"No, not really. I used to visit with my mother when I was little, and I do remember Edween Bistort, a loud kind of man. I saw Nessi sometimes. She was very sweet but my mother said she was quiet because she suffered from depression. I only saw Stann a couple of times."

"Just a final question if that's OK. One of the descriptions we have of Stann is that he had 'bionic eyes' what did they look like?" asked Enth.

"Stann designed his own prosthetic eyes. They look larger than normal eyes and they were designed so that he could attach farscopes or nearscopes directly to them which make his eyes look even bigger."

As Commander Enth left Bistort Tower he was surprised to see the stone steps clear of ice around the entrance. He was appalled by the waste of energy.

Chapter Three

THREEDAY

Enth forwarded his recording of the meeting with Sanda Bistort to Lalli Mak and then checked the three messages waiting for him.

0645 EST Interspace transmission from Space Commander Jaste Mars Colony to Enth Earth

<<NO REPLY FROM THE ALCHEMIST. FOUR HOURS TO DEADLINE. IF NOTHING FURTHER WILL SEND SHIP TO INTERCEPT AND DESTROY>>

Voice message from Investigator Mak to Enth

"Follow up on Stann's eyes. Professor Leo Manny who worked with the teenage Stann said that Stann's bionic eyes were 'like ordinary eyes but staring'; Professor Jen Jcke who worked on the universe scanning just before Stann was suspended said she only had a brief glimpse of him after the explosion when she called to collect equipment. She said his face 'looked sore' and his 'new prosthetic eyes were quite protuberant with thick lenses.'"

Digicom to Commander Enth from Admin Officer Claddis

<>

Commander Enth quickly went through the final Alchemist log message and could see how it added to their current information. Almost on cue, another message arrived from Mars.

0800 EST Interspace transmission from Space Commander Jaste Mars Colony to Governor Washh and Commander Enth Earth

<<ALCHEMIST HAS CHANGED COURSE. BISTORT MINING IS REFUSING TO HIRE US A SHIP. UNABLE TO INTERCEPT>>

This was just as a smug Commander Enth had been anticipating. He memmed Governor Washh and reassured him that appropriate action was in process.

0830 EST Mem to Lalli Mak

<<Read message from Jaste. Meeting my office 30 minutes>>

0900 Meeting with Enth and Mak

Enth greeted Mak as soon as she came through the door.

"I have promised to have a final report to Governor Washh before midday, and we should have enough time if we stay focussed. Firstly, give your review of Wendo's log entry and Sanda Bistort's statement then the final log entry will fit into a context."

"Right. OK. There are two main things that stick out for me" said Mak. "First of all Wendo's account of the structures on Verdant 3. Those green tubes and branched interconnected lattice are a machine of some kind, with the brown liquefied gel forced up the tubes and, I'm assuming, spraying down as rain. It's like a continuous motion device."

"Secondly, Stann's behaviour is really peculiar from the outset. After giving instructions to his team before the journey he then didn't talk to them at all, by Wendo's account, once they woke after stasis and went down onto the planet surface. That

193

scene in the clearing with the holo, I get a clue about from Sanda Bistort's information to you. I assume that he was setting up a little shrine to his sister. Was he expecting something on the planet to resurrect her? It's very weird. It's also quite confusing about his appearance. The bionic eyes fitted when he was young were similar to ordinary eyes, but then the explosion burnt his face so it looked 'sore' – and the prosthetic eyes he designed himself were quite protuberant with detachable lenses. I wonder which he wore under his spacesuit?" Then Mak added "So what about the final log entry?"

"It would be easy enough to conclude the worst scenarios from quite catastrophic events. But I think we will be able to see through smokescreens to reveal the truths about the journey of the Alchemist", said Enth, "I'll quickly review the brief log entry and then we can build answers."

"The final recording is again by Wendo on the ship and reporting conversations with Norris on the surface, the day after the last message, and there is a short addition by Rollo at the end."

He continued "Substantially the log report starts with the third day where Baris and Norris had been excavating the mineral cliff and Baris had identified what he thought was a brown crystalline ore containing several unusual isotopes of rare earth metals. After a day's work they had filled the ore trailer. Returning to the cabin to sleep they saw Stann assembling a large piece of equipment in another clearing ankle deep in the brown gel leaking from the poles he had broken. As they passed Stann switched on his superglide (was this to stop him sinking?) and his suit and the whole clearing flashed mirror bright. He didn't answer as they hailed him.

The rest of the log is from the day afterwards and Wendo's voice is garbled. She talks about an explosion and a huge pulse of light. Norris called her to report that Baris was dead, he had been thrown against the cliff. His suit was ripped and he had mineral extrusions growing down his back. Norris put Boris's body into the ore carrier and attached it to the Lander noting that Stann's boxes had already been stacked inside. He then gave instructions to Rolly to get the ship ready to go on his return. As for the final recording by Rolly, you should hear it in its entirety."

Planetfall Day 5. Recording by Rollo Desti, First Officer, the Alchemist.

(There was a sound of rasping breath and then a brief and final message):

Wendo and Norris are in the stasis boxes though both have mineral growths on their legs which may continue to develop past their knees during stasis. There has been no message from Stann so we assume he is dead. The ship is carrying Stann's and Wendo's samples and an ore trailer full of mineral ore from Verdant 3 and also Baris's body which Norris said is almost entirely mineralized. I may be hallucinating, but I thought I heard a rustling coming from Stann's large box. The ship's A1 senses movement but confirms only 3 biological entities with limited function.

The ship has return instructions programmed by Stann which he guaranteed would return us safely to the solar system. I cannot survive another stasis so I will be privileged to watch the stars until I die. I am making sure these ship recordings will be sent by the A1 as soon as the ship exits into normal space.

They both sat quietly for a short time. The image of Rolly watching the stars mesmerised them for a few minutes. Sitting opposite each other with eyes closed Enth's brain surged in synergy with Mak, perhaps there was a melding of synapses and prostheses: certainly a prolonged trance.

Suddenly Mak said loudly "So, transmutation was just a distraction"

"And firing the lasers was a significant action. But with unforeseen outcomes" said Enth,

"You go first." said Mak

"What was the purpose of the journey to Verdant 3? Stann Bistort wanted to go to Verdant 3 to re-animate his sister Nessi.

195

He theorised that the 'systematic particle instability' had the potential for replication when triggered by laser energy and—as it turned out-- catalysed by the brown gel. Whether this was re-animation using Nessi's DNA or 3D modelling of the holo image I'm not certain, said Enth. "but I am certain he didn't care about the ore mining or the science. Your turn now."

"What is the mechanism on the planet for? I know what this is," said Mak, "The key to understanding it was the heat. The planetary machine is a cooling system- gel sucked up the tubes, sprayed down as rain—cooling evaporation stopping the planet exploding. Stann has created a heat engine – the 'photon trace' became a 'space corridor'- – like a graviton mini black hole - – when he fired a laser BACK at Earth. I don't think he actually meant to leak heat via the energy gradient from a hot Verdant 3 to a cold Earth so finally giving away the whole secret as Bistort Towers heated up. I checked, the power grid could not have delivered that kind of voltage."

"What is the Alchemist carrying?" Mak also picked up on this one, "Following from your answer, the ship is carrying a dead Rolly and three wholly or partly mineralised crew. It's still possible but not likely that Norris and Wendo are still alive. And in a box there is a golem or automaton of Nessi. I bet the rustling was a parrot in the box as well.

The 'particle instability' makes Verdant 3 minerals contagious when triggered by the brown gel. (that appears to act as a 'Philosopher's Stone'). The ore carried by the alchemist is probably not active, but it would be too dangerous to take a risk..

"Whatever happened to Stannkenstein?" Enth was annoyed with himself for not guessing sooner, "Your point about Stann taking no interest in his team AND wondering about his prosthetic eyes fitting under his Space suit should have been enough, but it was Sanda Bistort's mistake about his eyes that confirmed it. She described his latest prosthesis which, had she been telling the truth about only seeing him when she was young, she couldn't have seen. Stann sent a Stann android to Verdant 3 and never left Earth at all. He stayed here waiting for his treasure from Verdant 3 to arrive on Mars and then get one of his ore carrier ships to bring it secretly to Earth. We will find Stann at Bistort Towers."

Commander Enth and Investigator Mak looked at each other's flushed face and their brains fizzed in unison. They each took out a Blue ExtraGel Ice Cap and put it on. Calm.

"But the ship needs intercepting" cried Mak, "What can be done as Mars Space Police have failed?"

"Already taken care of" said Commended Enth. "When the Governor passed the responsibility onto Mars Police it suddenly clicked. MarsOreMining Inc was Bistort Mining. They weren't going to let the Space Police destroy Stann Bistort's ship. So I asked Senior Officer Erl Trant to quietly take a Police Cruiser from Luna to intercept it. It is fitted with a much newer and faster version of the Krypton Thruster engine than the Alchemist and had a good chance of catching it, especially as it is now moving towards Earth. I'll send a message for an update."

"Now, let's collect a police escort and go to Bistort Towers and pick up Stann." Enth suggested.

Chapter Four

FIVEDAY

0900 EST Sky City. Office of Governor Washh

"Commander Enth and Investigator Mak. Thank you for your updates, and I note that Stann Bistort is now in custody. Perhaps we can be understanding about his incarceration if he can operate the heat tube to speed up the warming, and tell us how to follow the photon trace, if the scientists' agree it's wise, that is," said a flushed Governor Washh --he had needed to put the Ice Cap on when he thought the ship was to hit Earth and turn them all into quartz [as if it wasn't quartz already] and continued:

"We can breathe a sigh of relief now that Space Police Officer Erl Trant has confirmed the destruction of the Alchemist and all its dangerous cargo and made arrangements with the Near Earth Monitoring Station to collect the debris, and shoot the drone out away from Earth."

Enth and Mak exchanged looks of wide eyed innocence.

Chapter Five

THE NEXT THREEDAY

Governor Washh delivered his live news update on the intercommsnet and concluded, "The Council Ministers have agreed to give Medals of Valour and 5,000 energy credits each to the three heroic Space Police. The council has also agreed posthumous medals and commemorative statues for the two brave astronauts who lost their lives. We are pleased to announce that Scientist Wendo Storr and Captain Tod Norris are recovering well after reconstructive surgery at Bistort Centre, MarsPort."

Admiral Enth and Commander Mak stood side by side watching the vid. Blue EatraGel Ice Caps on, holding hands.

"So where did Erl Trant leave the samples from Verdant 3 then?"

"It seems that Bistort MarsOreMining Inc's exploration team have brought back an unknown Erbium-Gold-Terbium Ore. Coincidently Erl Trant is to become the new Chief Pilot of Bistort Exploration"

"So you're telling me that Stannkenstein did discover transmutation?"

"Who knows? But if Erl Trant can bring back more exotic rare metal ore, he will be made Partner of Bistort Mining Inc. How do you fancy being a partner of a Governor, Admiral Enth?"

"I'd need a bigger Blue ExtraGel Ice Cap."

About the Author

Mary Latham's father's bookshop provided unlimited opportunities to foster a reading addiction, starting with many series of story books (until the authors ran out of steam), through the Eagle Comic, non-fiction science books, sci-fi and the New Scientist, and, if all else failed, sauce bottles. She studied Physics and Chemistry and trained to be a Science Teacher.

She has a Master of Education degree from the University of Manchester (amongst other stuff) and undertaken a lot of educational research projects, (including studies of neurodivergence and reading) with a plethora of published reports and articles. This kept her busy, if not always entirely thrilled, for years.

As well as writing science fiction stories she is just completing a pre-teen/young adult sci-fantasy adventure trilogy.

Thank-you for Reading

If you had as much pleasure reading my book as I did in writing it, I hope you can leave me a review on Amazon so that others can find this story.

Not only is knowing what you think really important and interesting for me, but it also helps other readers work out whether they would like it too.

Do visit my website and find out about the latest news, competitions and free offers.

www.marylathambooks.co.uk

Printed in Great Britain
by Amazon

37932166R00118